For Dave,
Good friend of a good
friend, and what could
be better than that?
Dream your life
& live your
dreams..."
M Murdoch

MURDER IN LA PAZ

A Rick Sage Mystery

MURDOCH HUGHES

Hard Shell Word Factory

For Jan, who is everything.

ISBN: 0-7599-3479-7
Trade Paperback
Published May 2004

© 2004 Murdoch Hughes
eBook ISBN: 0-7599-3478-9
Published April 2004

Hard Shell Word Factory
PO Box 161
Amherst Jct. WI 54407
books@hardshell.com
www.hardshell.com
Cover art © 2004 Mary Z. Wolf

Chapter One

"FIFTY-SEVEN," I SHOUTED, watching Antiay's naked body submerge and resurface as she turned to begin lap fifty-eight. I was counting laps for her as she swam a hundred in the pool, but I was having a hard time keeping track, being mesmerized by her body sliding through blue water with the wake closing over the tan lines on her buttocks. And those turns...with the quick flashes of places I had spent the afternoon sliding in and along and through. It was enough to make a guy write poetry, although the lines I came up with wouldn't make it past a congressional censor. What the heck, this is Mexico. "Fifty-uh-eight," I stammered. Censors be damned. This was pure poetry.

It had been a wonderful siesta. We had carried the mattress out to the deck overlooking the pool, surrounded on three sides by an arbor of purple, pink, and red bougainvillea; with roses, jasmine, and honeysuckle tossed in, and topped off with newly ripened grapes we'd picked and fed each other during breaks. If there is a heaven it's got to be—

"Sixty-nine," I called out, a little late on the turn.

Antiay stopped and swam toward me, laughing. "Rick, since when does sixty-nine come after fifty-eight?" She slapped the water, and cool spray splashed me.

"It's the only number I could think of."

"That's okay. It's a good number to end on. There's no way I'm doing a hundred today; you wore me out. Besides, it's late and I have to go."

I jumped up, dove in with a tight turn and swam back to her. She threw her arms around my neck, and as we kissed I released my grip on the edge of the pool and we slid under together.

She came up laughing. "Rick, I love you," she said, her eyes twinkling. "But you're making it awful hard to leave."

"Yes, I know. I'm always the last one out of the movie theater, and I love reading trilogies because they last so long. And you, I just can't get enough of."

She boosted herself up on the side of the pool. "I'm sorry Rick, I hate to go, too. But I have to meet someone and I don't want to be late." She stood up, grabbed the bath towel from the deck chair and dried herself. The sun was low in the sky and it was already starting to cool off. She wrapped the first towel around her, picked up a second and hung her head over, drying her long blond hair.

I watched. "Yeah well, that's another thing. We've known each other for months and I still don't know that much about you. I mean, I know you, but I don't know how you became you. I'm supposed to be a detective, so how do you imagine that makes me feel? You won't tell me who you're going to see? Maybe it's some other guy."

"Why, you are a detective, aren't you? This afternoon was just a warm-up. I'm really quite excited and I can't wait to get to that big, beautiful hunk of man I'm going to meet."

I leaped out of the pool and went for her. "We detectives have ways of dealing with people like you," I said as she made like a tamer of wild beasts, stretching her towel out to snap me. I feinted, she missed, and I took her in my arms. We were both laughing, but the sounds faded to smiles as we responded to each other once again. We kissed, but she pushed herself away, her eyes sad.

"Rick, I'm sorry. I'll tell you everything, but it has to be when I'm ready. It's very difficult, for me as much as it is for you. I'm still not over it...I...I have to work it out in my own way. But soon, I promise you, soon." She pulled me close and kissed me again, her lips seasoned with the taste of her tears.

"I'm sorry, Antiay," I said, leaning back so I could see her blue eyes. "I promised no questions. It's the bad habits of a private detective. I guess I don't know when I've got it made. Go ahead and punch me in the nose."

She smiled. "No, I wouldn't do that. It's battered enough. I love this nose," and she kissed it as I wiped the tears from her cheeks. "I really do have to get dressed."

"Okay hon, I'll see you later." I pulled on my jeans as she disappeared into the house. Then I walked to the poolside bar and mixed myself a *Cuba Libre*.

I was sipping it by the pool when she appeared in the doorway for an instant and waved. "Goodbye, Rick. I'm late. I'll see you for dinner."

"Don't say goodbye, say *hasta luego*," I replied, but she was already gone. "Never, ever say goodbye," I whispered to the honeysuckle and the blood-red bougainvillea.

I WAS IN an extremely good mood as I parked my Harley near the restaurant where we planned to have dinner. Walking the two blocks to Antiay's apartment, I whistled part of a Mexican love song that kept replaying in my mind.

We'd had a full afternoon of great sex, and soon we'd be eating lobsters as we rubbed knees and watched the boats riding at anchor in *La Paz* harbor. What more could a man desire? Ah, Mexico. Beautiful, sweet Mexico.

Her apartment was really just a room in an old rundown hotel, and I'd been trying to get her to move in with me. But she valued her independence and, to tell the truth, so did I. Besides, though the room was cheap, it was adequate, and on her hourly wage as an English teacher she couldn't afford anything else. It was obvious she'd once had plenty of money because poverty didn't affect her like it does someone who's endured it for years. It was freedom and "being on her own," she said she valued most right now. Her beautiful, blue eyes lit up when she talked about her freedom, and I knew she'd escaped from some oppressive situation, though she never wanted to talk about her past. I figured it was a bad marriage, but she never said and I tried not to ask. Besides, the timing was perfect. Right now we both wanted to live and love in the present.

I noticed the unmarked police car parked next to the *Exquisito* hot dog stand, where every night, Alberto, the sleepy vendor, staked out the corner in front of the hotel. Working two or three jobs to support a large family, he grabbed what winks he could, nodding off between customers. The aroma got to me and I thought about grabbing a quick dog for an appetizer. I glanced back at the police car. It was a white Ford with a two-way radio antenna, and something about the way it had been hastily parked aroused the detective in me. I sensed something was wrong and my stomach churned. The two stories of hotel rooms were built around an inner courtyard, and I hurried past the unoccupied check-in desk, looking up at Antiay's second-story room.

My heart skipped and I felt dizzy when I saw her open door and the manager standing on the mezzanine next to it, staring down at me horror-stricken, like he'd seen something terrible.

I took the stairs two at a time and ran to the open doorway. The manager grabbed my arm as he shouted, "No, *Señor*, no!"

I shook him off and stepped into the doorway, where two cops standing inside blocked me. I pushed past, handing them my wallet. I guess they decided it would be more interesting to watch my reaction than it would be to try to stop me.

I felt sick, but I tried to act cool, like the professional I was supposed to be. I even tried to pretend it was just another crime scene.

But the cool melted when I saw the body. She was face down on the bed. Not exactly face down...because when I pushed aside her blonde hair, there was no face.

One of the cops shouted something in Spanish that was probably their version of some cop thing like, don't touch the evidence, but they needn't have bothered. I stumbled backward. My hand found the telephone and dialed Freddy's number all by itself.

"Freddy, it's me Rick," I said into the mouthpiece when I heard his voice. "Listen! I need your help...I'm at Antiay's apartment...she's been shot...she's dead...get over here right away, will you? I need an interpreter."

He muttered something about "hanging in there," and I mumbled back, "Yeah, I'll try—*gracias*."

I hung up the damn phone. Slammed it down, without meaning to, and the loud bang startled me. My brain was sending my body confused signals. I felt weak and my muscles were over-compensating or something. Sweat streamed off me, but I felt cold as a margarita. My dry lips tasted the salt of tears.

I had to get a hold of myself. I'd seen dead bodies before, and besides, the body wasn't her. The body was just another murder victim— an object, like an expensive piece of broken furniture.

Involuntarily, I glanced again at the corpse on the bed, hoping it wouldn't be there.

It was there all right, and my stomach churned buttermilk. My legs stumbled weak-kneed to the open window and I puked my guts out. I heard the cops laughing behind me, and I wanted to choke them, but instead I clutched the windowsill, retching some more, struggling to understand what was happening.

This was a nightmare. Time seemed all out of whack. Could it have been less than two hours since we'd been together? How could it be that Antiay and I, now, were Antiay and I, then? We were supposed to be having dinner right now. This couldn't be us.

Vomit dripped down my chin and the detective in me started to take over. Oh yeah, always the damn detective. I wanted it all to be a mistake, but stumbling to the window to puke, I'd noticed the silver bracelet I'd given her...on the wrist dangling from the left side of the blood-soaked mattress.

Someone handed me a rag and I wiped my mouth. But I had no strength. The cool breeze felt good. Maybe if I closed my eyes...no, that was bad—the red was too much like blood. I stared through a dying palm tree outside the window. Stall, stall. You need time to recover. It's just another dead body. Forget her, she's not here. There'll be time for pain later. Think of something else. Anything. What am I doing here? Jesus I'm tired. Yeah, that's for sure...real tired.

A tired private eye, lately of Los Angeles. I was especially tired of murder, which is why I moved here. A nice quiet little town. A perfect place to do nothing but spend time in the sun, reading and maybe writing again. Scribble poems and sip margaritas by the pool. Let old wounds heal. Get a tan for the first time in my life, because in my line, florescent tubes are as close as you come to the light of day. The alley cat's last howl just before dawn is your sweet goodnight...Oh God! Antiay!

I mentally shook myself. Don't think about it! Put one thought in front of the other and keep moving....

Yeah I was tired. Tired of the color red. Blood red. Most people don't know blood comes in shades. Seeping onto a white shirt from a lung shot, it's bright red. But before the victim in death's landscape stops jiggling, the red begins to darken until, say the body isn't found for three days, the blood dries to almost a dark brown. In the bad light of cheap hotels anyway.

I call it "still life in a pool," as in pool of blood, but it'll never be hung in some mansion of the rich and bored. That's because they paint their own bloody landscapes. Only with a different medium. They're painted in the rainbow light of crystal chandeliers, and the canvas is the plushest carpet money can buy.

But dead is dead, and I was tired of the rich, too. They're always shocked when reality intrudes on their fantasies. Very shocked indeed when I'm the reality; two hundred pounds of muscle well-packed on a six-foot three-inch frame, holding a chrome-plated forty-five cannon in one hand and dangling a set of chrome-plated handcuffs in the other. It's funny, because you could see the process in their faces. Like a cartoon double take. One second reality hits, and the next second they're trying to turn it back into fantasy. The handcuffs become Tiffany bracelets, and I'm the butler and would I please get this mess cleaned up. There's a good tip in it for me.

Sure it's a cliché, but I couldn't resist telling them, with a smile, "There are some things money can't buy."

One day I realized even my sense of humor was getting jaded. So I came down here to La Paz, a quiet Mexican town near the tip of Baja, because some jerk told me it was too small for big-time crime. Yeah sure! Tell that to the blonde in the still life in a pool. The blonde who just an hour ago washed off my hot scent in a cold shower, took a swim and walked out my front door, forever. Like an unfinished poem.

Murder doesn't rhyme for me.

Strange the things that run through your mind at a time like this. Like poetry—

"Are you all right Rick?"

Like Antiay—

"Rick, are you okay, *mi amigo?*"

Like blood-red sunsets—

"Rick, hey, snap out of it, *amigo*, this is—"

"Leave me alone," I snarled. I didn't want to snap out of it...to turn away from the window...from that dying palm tree out there swaying in the last gasp of tonight's *Coromuel*, the dry southerly wind blowing the heat off this desert town by the sea. Blowing like the breeze from the fly-specked ceiling fan drying blood which once flowed beneath soft skin. Blood-red, like the haze descending over me....

"Rick! This is serious shit here! These are *federales*...very serious *federales!*" the voice hissed in my ear. "They want some answers, and they want them now!"

The far-away voice I was hearing belonged to my friend, Fast Freddy. And that meant this wasn't some bad dream. Real life is scarier than dreams and much bloodier. It takes years before you no longer puke. Tonight was the first time in a long time for me, and not wanting it on their spit-shined boots, the *federales* had backed off to give me some time to recover in the cool breeze of the *Coromuel*.

But now the dogs were snarling—backed up by machine-gun questions in Spanish, directed at my pal, who had the unlucky job of Mexican interpreter to a *gringo* murder suspect. Their questions were directed to Freddy, but aimed at a bull's-eye they'd already painted on me.

"They want to know why you killed her." Fast Freddy interpreted, a tremble developing in his usually Kahlua-smooth voice, as he edged away from me.

I couldn't blame him for wanting some distance between us. Don't stand under a tree in a lightning storm is damned sound advice. Still, this tree had weathered a lot of storms.

Cops were cops, though, even nasty ones like these two brutes. I knew from experience, when a cop goes for the jugular—it means they smell blood. I had to show them some red meat other than my own or I was headed for a grungy cell. In this country, there's no revolving-door system. It's easy enough to get thrown in, but you pay hell getting out. They call it Napoleonic justice. Guilty until proven innocent. Once arrested, that is.

So I stood tall and gave them my Very-Important-*Gringo* look. Insulted, mad as hell, and upset at the death of a close friend. I'd seen the movie dozens of times. I had to play Bogart under interrogation. I looked them in the eye and coolly spoke to Freddy.

"Tell them I didn't kill her. That we were close friends, and I am a close friend of the governor. In fact, I was with him tonight while this crime was taking place, and he will vouch for me. Tell them also that the governor will be unhappy if they waste time arresting a friend when they should be looking for the murderer. Tell them I won't leave town because I want to find the killer more than they do. Tell them I am very upset and tired, but I know nothing about this crime, so I would like to go home and rest. If they wish, I will make a statement tomorrow. Tell them to arrest me or let me go."

A moment of silence passed as Fast Freddy placed his bet. But when he finally interpreted my speech the tremble in his voice was gone and it sounded like pure, sweet, *Don Pedro* Kahlua once again. I knew then I had at least a draw, which was as good as a win.

When Freddy finished, there was a pause as the dogs pulled back from my throat. They exchanged a glance and a shrug before the one on my right growled. But in English this time, tricky fellow.

"Okay *Señor*, you go for now. Do not leave town please. We may wish to speak with you more."

"*Bueno.*" I shrugged and walked out the door. Fast Freddy followed saying, "*Muy amable, muy amable, gracias,*" to the officers as he passed.

Muy amable means very kind in Spanish. I didn't argue the point, but very kind was not the way I'd describe those guys. And very kind was definitely not how they were going to treat me if they made a point of contacting the governor right away. I was banking on the lateness of the hour and the reluctance of the *policiá* to disturb a high official who might be drunk in front of his satellite TV. But it was a gamble. High officials don't like to be surprised by cold, hard facts in the morning, either. Particularly if that cold, hard fact was a corpse with an international incident tag on her toe.

So Freddy and I two-stepped down the exit stairs and out the door while I counted the lies and half-lies I'd told the *federales*, and schemed how I could juggle them all into some kind of story that might hold together better than a soggy taco.

Freddy jogged beside me as I headed to the *Malecón*, the stone-wall street along the beach, where I knew one of the few working pay phones in La Paz was located. He knew we needed to put some space between us and the *federales*. Freddy was quick about things like that. But if he'd known our freedom depended on someone at the governor's Palace putting through a late night call from a *gringo*, he'd have booked town, not stopping this side of Los Angeles. Luckily he didn't ask.

Chapter Two

WHEN WE REACHED the pay telephone, Freddy tried to ask a few of the questions buzzing around in his head like killer bees. That was fair enough. He sensed his way of life was on the line, and he was right. I stalled him with a wave of my hand, because if this phone call didn't get through we'd both have a long time to ponder questions. What we needed right now were answers.

I dropped the coin and dialed the number. It seemed half of eternity before a woman's voice spoke to me, in Spanish, from the other end. I jumped in with both size-thirteen feet.

"Listen to me. I know you speak English because I talked to you two days ago. My name is Rick Sage. I'm a friend of the governor and I have to speak to him. Tell him a *gringa* has been murdered and I have some information he should know, unless he wants to be implicated in a very nasty international incident. Do you have that? Okay, I'll hold on."

I heard her telephone clunk when she laid it on the desk, and I pondered my speech while I waited. Sure I had lied to the *federales*. But one thing I told them wasn't a lie. I am a friend of the governor. Or at least I was until tonight. He was one of the jerks who told me there was no big-time crime in La Paz. Politicians lie, and I knew that. I'm a big boy so I can hardly hold lying against him. We all lie when we have to.

The gov owed me a favor. It's a long story, but the short version is, I'd saved his son from involvement with some nasty cocaine-ring characters up in the States a few years back. The kid had been somewhat innocent—not totally—but enough that I didn't want to wreck his future. So I'd driven him to Tijuana and put him on a plane home. Turned out he had a good relationship with his dad and told the old man the whole story. That was the beginning of a warm friendship between the gov and me. But was it warm enough to get me out of this mess? I didn't know.

"That you, Rick?" The voice in my ear startled me.

"Yeah, it's me."

"What kind of *cabrón* message was that?"

His voice was clear and unslurred. That was good at least.

"Sorry to bother you, but I need a favor. A very big favor."

"Yes, go on," he replied, rather coldly I thought, but then I had mentioned murder.

"To make it short, a *gringa* friend of mine was murdered tonight. I didn't do it but the *policiá* ran into me at the scene, and they suspect me. I used your name to keep from being arrested. In fact I said I was with you tonight at the time of the murder. I can get another alibi, but I'd like you to say I was with you until six o'clock. That's before the murder was committed. I know because I was with her then and—"

"And you didn't kill her, right?" he interrupted. "Because I can get you out of the country now. But later is out of the question."

"Damn it! I didn't kill her and I intend to stay around to prove it."

"Okay *amigo*," said my friend. But the politician's voice went on. "But don't contact me until this is over. There's nothing more I can do for you."

"*Gracias Señor*," I said into a dead phone line. The bloodstains weren't even dry and already I'd used most of my big chips. This was going to be a tough game and I'd have to play my cards carefully from here on out. Well, I always kept an ace or two up my sleeve.

I turned to the street and the world suddenly went into stop action as I noticed the car. Freddy was saying, "What was that all about Rick? You mean you weren't with—"

It was as if someone turned up the dial on my senses. Way up. I saw the open window, the black hole of the gun muzzle, then the flame and the sound of the shot and the bullet burning a path between us...the decay and saltwater smell of the beach invaded my senses as the bullet barely missed my ear...then the roar of the engine, and squealing tires, and Freddy ending the sentence he'd started milliseconds ago, with the frightened non sequitur, "What the fucking *mierda?*"

It wasn't like in the movies. In the movie, I'd have knocked Freddy out of the way, ducked, and snapped off a few shots, maybe wounding one of the bad guys as the rear window glass shattered. Maybe I'd even hit the driver and the car would careen out of control and smash into the trunk of the old Laurel of India tree. Yeah, and the dead body would lay on the horn as a warning to other malcontents intent on taking on the old gunslinger.

But there had been no time for the brain to signal the muscles, no chance to pull out the gun, and not even a license plate to read. There was only the stop-action scene, and dead or not dead. The rest was trails of light. People do get killed in war. Even the would-be hero. I was alive because they'd missed. The question was, did they intend to? If so, they'd nearly botched the job. Nobody in real life can come that close, firing a handgun from a moving car. Not even me. But it was an important question nonetheless and I—

Freddy interrupted my train of thought by clamping me on the shoulder, and I remembered he had been missed, too. He looked very pale for someone from the sub-tropics.

"We gotta book, *amigo*," he sighed, more than a bit relieved at not being a corpse. "This night is *muy malo*. You will explain *mañana, si?*"

He was jogging down the street when I called out, "*La Posada* for breakfast."

He waved without looking back as I jogged off in the opposite direction.

TO BE SEEN in the vicinity of two shooting incidents in one night is as good as guilty to a cop in any country. No one else had been in the street when the gun went off, but that didn't guarantee someone hadn't heard the shot and reported it. The night's proceedings aside, La Paz was still innocent enough that a gunshot wasn't likely to go unnoticed. I jogged to the corner and turned it, then slowed to a walk. Running was another come-on to the cops, and my motorcycle was only two blocks away.

I reached my hog, fired her up, and roared away in the opposite direction of the pay phone on the *Malecón*. I was breaking my cardinal rule of always letting the hog warm up before taking off, but necessity is the mother of all rules. And I figured that once I was moving I could always claim the shot was the backfire of my bike, even though a backfire didn't happen with this Harley, bad fuel or not. I kept her too sharp for that.

As I rode down the dark streets I added 'no warm-up for the hog' to my grudge list against whoever was responsible for this night's chaos. My hogster was barely one year old—hardly broken in yet. Just a couple thousand miles around Los Angeles and the eight hundred miles and change down the Baja. Add several hundred miscellaneous miles since the trip, running the one hundred miles over to Cabo San Lucas a few times to do the town with Antiay—

Oh man, there's that pain again. That twisted dagger in my heart wired directly to my brain.

Antiay. I hadn't even started to mourn Antiay. Real men do cry, and tears flowed down my cheeks. I wiped them away and tasted them, biting my hand. Strange. They tasted like blood.

I knew the taste of blood. I knew the taste of tears, too, but it had been a long time. You train yourself not to notice either until you're safely alone. I guess my subconscious had made that decision for me. I was alone on the hog with Antiay's spirit hugging me close from behind like she used to.

Somehow the Harley found the open highway toward Cabo, and the speedometer pushed past one hundred. The Cardón cactus blurred in the moonlight, like cemetery headstones through tears. Oh I was wounded all right—by the same bullet that entered her skull from behind and blasted her beauty all over the wall of that cheap hotel room. Her blood and my tears streaming out of one giant wound; a death wound for her, an open wound for me that wouldn't heal without the salve of revenge.

I twisted the throttle farther and the speedometer nicked one hundred and ten. It was going to take a hard ride to dry these tears, and if somehow I didn't come back in one piece, well, that was going to save me a lot of trouble. I felt the low rumble of the wild hog like a primal growl in my gut, and I rode on into the night.

Chapter Three

EXHAUSTED, I'D RUMBLED home in the dark just before dawn. I guess I stumbled onto the bed, clothes and all, because that's how I woke up, sweating from a bad dream of being chased by faceless zombies reciting Shakespeare. I tried but couldn't remember the lines. Too bad. The best clues came from dreams sometimes. The subconscious is a damn good detective. It's not squeamish or sentimental like the conscious mind.

Separating the dream from other memories of last night was difficult—including the ride into purgatory where I'd delivered Antiay's soul and begun to sort out the bloody threads dangling from the mystery of her death. I felt if I pulled on the right one the whole thing would begin to unravel. There was something not quite right, and on the ride home I almost had it. But in my misery the clue had faded, and now at ten in the bright light of morning, all I really knew for sure were two things: Antiay had been murdered, and I had to find her killer.

I stepped into the cold shower and tried to shock myself out of the daze I was in. What I needed now were some cold, hard facts. There were things going on in this town that had stirred my curiosity even before someone had murdered Antiay. But I had ignored them except in the most casual way. Of course asking questions was second nature to me, and I had asked Antiay and Freddy and others about them. But I had been trying to get away from the detective life, and when I hadn't gotten satisfactory answers I'd just filed it away under: Who cares?

But now I did care. Sure, it was possible Antiay's death was the work of some psycho-punk, but I didn't think so. Call it intuition, or a detective's hunch, or even an over-active imagination fed by an ego that couldn't accept Antiay being murdered by accident. I had a strong feeling her death was part of some greater mystery.

It was partly the fact that I had known very little about her background. She'd kept secrets from me with the promise that some day she'd tell me everything, but to please trust her now.

It hadn't been easy for me, but I'd told myself it didn't matter. We were in love. Every time the nagging questions had surfaced I reburied them. Now they were rising again, and I realized I'd always sensed her connection to some things that had been bothering me.

Like why were there so many Germans in this town? Antiay is a

German name, but she seemed to consciously avoid contact with the expatriated German community. And the old hotel being refurbished over on the Mogote—a desert peninsula of mesquite and sand that forms the other side of La Paz Bay—that was run by Germans. The hotel had attracted my bloodhound nose for unusual scents, even before Antiay's murder. Once a detective always a detective, and I never could resist poking my nose into something that didn't seem quite right. The old hotel had never made any money it seemed, and with half the world economy in recession the prospects didn't seem any better now. Out of curiosity and that relentless itching for everything to make sense, to have a logical explanation, I'd been asking questions about the place for weeks. Casually, of course. It really had been none of my business. Just old habits I couldn't suppress. But what few answers I got only made me itchier. Now, the German question had me scratching like I was wearing wool underwear made in Berlin.

Another mystery that had me itching was the story of the multi-million dollar private yacht anchored in the harbor. It didn't make sense because La Paz wasn't the kind of big money tourist town that attracted those kinds of people. Sure, La Paz is a wonderful place, but it has no nightlife, and no fabulous restaurants on the scale the rich required. Yeah, we have *Asadero Hery's*, the best *carne asada* taco stand in all of Mexico, but Hery is his own head waiter and you have to take your turn at the picnic tables. You see what I mean. And the yacht had been here during two of the best months for anchoring off Acapulco, or Mazatlán, or even Cabo San Lucas. Maybe there was a perfectly good explanation—if so I'd find it. Otherwise...I'd find that, too.

The gossip was a rich German owned the yacht. Antiay and I had been walking along the Malecón as it first steamed into the harbor. When I'd pointed it out I was sure she turned pale. Then she'd changed the subject with a hug, diverting my attention from boats to bed. That worked, except later I'd asked Freddy about the yacht. He hadn't known anything except the German ownership rumor. Now I was determined to find out the rest.

Another itch tickling my detective's nose was the high-powered cigarette-type speedboat that had "Parasail" painted in English all over it. Of course all of the big tourist towns had those boats pulling tourists around the bay while they dangled from a parasail at a height of a hundred and fifty feet. Tourists are funny like that. They'd flock to the *palapa* bar offering the cheapest double *Margaritas* made with half cheap tequila and half grain alcohol, then they'd pay big bucks to have their crotch ripped out hanging from a parasail. And of course the Mexicans loved to go,

"Oops!" and drop them in the sea or drag them face-first across the beach. I would, too. What people won't do if someone tells them it's fun. But my point is, those high powered boats are expensive, and expensive to maintain. There just aren't enough big-spending tourists in La Paz to support that kind of business. In the few months it had been anchored here, I'd only seen it flying its parasail a few times. And my cynical nose told me that might be for show.

Several other itches had to be scratched, too, I thought as I finished toweling off and began shaving. I wondered if the German presence and the yacht had anything to do with the increased U.S. Drug Enforcement Agency presence I'd noticed around La Paz. You could spot a DEA snooper like a birthday clown at a tea party. He'd corner you in a bar and buddy up to you real quick, all the while acting like a newcomer tourist asking endless questions. Then not-so-subtly he'd start talking about cocaine and all the great parties he'd been to in other party places. It was a routine agents learned in drug school kindergarten and some of them never got past the first grade.

I don't care much for the Federal Narc Squad. I guess it shows. Sure it's a dirty job and somebody's got to do it. That's the problem. It attracts a certain type of shark-like person. They'd set up their own mothers for a promotion. And they have an attitude. Very self-righteous. They'd let a killer go free in order to bust a small-time marijuana operation. I know. I'd seen it happen. The Agent in charge of that case was Bill White, who is now DEA Honcho for all of Mexico. Yeah, and guess what? I saw him here in La Paz two days ago. We go way back, but I'd piss on his leg if I got the chance.

Maybe I'm old-fashioned. I believe crimes against children are the worst offenses. Then comes murder and rape, and there are several categories of those. Saving people from themselves doesn't seem like it should be high on the list. Most of the harm to society is created by the illegality of drugs. If you rate crime, narcotics has got to be somewhere down below white-collar crimes like executives who steal old people's life savings, and the politicians they all pay off one way or another. On second thought maybe that whole bunch is as bad as murderers and rapists. And there are the crimes that aren't even illegal because the people making the laws profit from them. I don't know, it's complicated and I'm no philosopher. For me, it's murder. That's the crime I've always taken personally—even before Antiay became a victim. I have my reasons.

Anyway, with a dead body appearing around the time Scumbag White arrives in town, I had to mark it down high on my list of unusual coincidences. I believe in coincidence about as much as I believe in honest politicians and the cavalry to the rescue. I'd rather bet a long-shot in the last race.

I knew there were other angles to consider, but the list I had by the time I'd finished my morning chores was enough to get me started. Besides, no matter the reason for Antiay's murder, if I stirred up this pot of questions, people would get anxious to give me some kind of answer. A lie can give you a lot more questions to ask, while the truth answers at least one.

I had to get going if I was going to make the few blocks to the *La Posada* before Freddy gave up on me. I was already overdue on the average thirty minutes I was usually late for appointments. Yeah, well, Freddy was always at least twenty minutes late himself. Did that make me on time somewhere in the Universe? Hell, I don't know. It's all too complicated. I slipped on my black cotton bowling shirt, for mourning, and ducked out through the lipstick red bougainvillea.

I WALKED UP to the *La Posada de Englebert*. What a horrible name for a beautiful place. Up until a month ago it had been plain old *La Posada*, which means "The Inn." Then Englebert Humperdink, the American pop-singer, bought the place. They'd already changed the half-circle, wrought-iron logo over the entrance gate from *La Posada* to *La Posada de Englebert*. In Mexico the name "*la posada*" takes on a religious meaning around Christmas because of the manger at "the Inn" where Jesus was born, so you've got to wonder who in the heck this Humperdink character thinks he is.

In any case, it isn't much in the way of a hotel. It's okay on a tight budget. It has a pool and the rooms are quaint, clean, little boxes with little fake-fireplaces, but it will never attract the big-money crowd. So why did the Humperdink group buy it? Another of those pesky questions.

While the rooms are modest, the restaurant is world-class with a world-class view. You look out through the palm trees around the pool and the *Palapa* bar, to the bright blue of La Paz Bay, and across that to the Mesquite trees of the Mogote. You can even make out the white walls of the old hotel over there I had questions about.

But later for that. As I entered the gates of the single-story *La Posada*, my mind was on the food. Roberto, the chef, had been head-chef for some of the best restaurants in Mexico City, but the pollution, crime (Oh Antiay), and major-city hustle had finally become too much for him. A few years back he had discovered the peace of La Paz, and when you consider La Paz means peace, well... he found what he was looking for. He'd been at the *La Posada* ever since.

Roberto specialized in collecting the best recipes from different cities, villages, and geographic areas of Mexico. Freddy swore the *Sopa de Lima*—a tangy bowl of soup made with chicken, giblets and vegetables, and flavored with the unusual sour lime of the *Yucatan*—took him back to a steamy night in *Chetumal* on the *Yucatan* Peninsula when he was just nineteen. Even now, he says, in spite of eight intervening years and many loves, when he tastes Roberto's *Sopa de Lima* he can feel her lips and inhale the salt scent of the sea in her hair.

Yes, well, I've never had such luck with the *Sopa de Lima*. Sure, it's a great soup, but after Freddy's description, when I tried my first bowl-full I was prepared for the napkin to become an umbrella tent on my lap. I guess you had to be there in the Yucatan at nineteen.

Maybe the soup was that good, but without telling Freddy, I suspect the passion of youth and lust in the tropics had much to do with it.

I saw Freddy waiting at our usual table near the pool and joined him. He wore an expensive blue silk suit with a T-shirt. He'd watched too many Miami Vice re-runs on his satellite TV, but what could you say? He was addicted to fancy clothes, women, and cars.

"*Hola, amigo,*" he said as I sat down. "*Cómo estás?*"

"I'm fine," I replied. "How are you, my friend?"

"*Bien, gracias,*" he responded as the waiter filled my coffee cup.

I was learning Spanish but I was still hesitant to use it. There's something about being a grown person talking with a preschool vocabulary that's hard to get over. Besides, Freddy's English was much better than my Spanish. Of course I should have learned more before I ever came down here. Fortunately, most Mexicans forgive your ignorance as long as you make an effort...in spite of the occasional *gringo* tourist who's insulted if a Mexican doesn't speak English. Ah, the language barrier—much more formidable than a mere river.

I examined Freddy's face for the effects of the previous night's events. The anxiety was there all right. "You don't look so good Freddy. About like I feel. Pass the cream, will you?"

He passed the cream. "What happened Rick? Who would—"

He dropped the rest of the question as the waiter approached again. "The usual *Señor?*"

"Yeah sure. *Chilaquiles, dos huevos* on the side, *jugo de naranja,* and *tortillas de harina. Gracias.*" The waiter nodded and headed for the kitchen. I wasn't hungry, but I had to go through the motions, putting one foot in front of the other....

Freddy waited for a response while I sipped my coffee. Ah caffeine. "I don't have a clue what happened last night, Freddy. All I have are questions. You know I came down here to get away from this shit. Then the first and only corpse I stumble over just happens to be the body of a very close friend. What a coincidence! Yeah, I got lots of questions. Can you help me find some answers?"

"Sure...maybe...my friend. If you can answer me one question."

I looked up at him from my coffee, surprised at the tone of his voice. "What?"

"Why the *federales?*"

"What do you mean?" Then it hit me. "*Federales*," I mumbled. Christ, that was it—one of the things that had been bothering me about last night that I couldn't quite dig out. *Federales*, or the Federal Judicial Police, would only be there if illegal drugs were involved. Murder would be handled by the Municipal Police or the State Judicial Police. "*Federales!*" I said again. "They got there first. Just before me...they barely beat me to the scene...Yeah, I see Freddy. Why?"

Freddy's face showed he had already been down this avenue of thought. While I'd been mourning Antiay, he'd been asking tough questions. That's what emotion does to a detective—like a hard blow to the gut, it knocks the wind out of you and all you can think about is one more breath.

"Yes, my friend," he went on, leading me along. "They were sent by someone. But they found no drugs at the scene—otherwise they'd never have let us go, Governor or no. It was meant to be a trap. But why? Was she involved with *drogas*, Rick?"

"What the fuck's the matter with you? She was a damn schoolteacher!"

Freddy shrugged, and I knew my protest sounded hollow.

I felt the resolve drain out of me along with my appetite. Maybe I didn't want to know the answers this time. The waiter brought our breakfast. Freddy had ordered earlier, but he didn't look hungry either. I slid the eggs onto the *chilaquiles* out of habit. I stared at them for a moment, and they stared back at me. Huge, dead, yellow eyes. I began to eat them anyway. Life...goes on.

While we ate, I told Freddy some of the angles I wanted to look into—particularly, information about the million-dollar yacht, and the reason for the increased DEA presence.

"I'll see what I can do," he replied. "But you've got to be straight with me, Rick. I don't want to get between the *federales* and any drug business. You know what I mean?"

"Yeah Freddy, I know what you mean. I'll try to give you plenty of room to cover your ass if it comes to that. All I want you to do is ask around—and maybe get me aboard that yacht. But...officially...I've just hired you to interpret for me. Okay?"

"Okay, *amigo*. You understand...I'm not used to this heavy-duty stuff. I don't care nothing about being shot at. I've had a couple *cabrón* husbands pretty mad at me. But murder and maybe *drogas*...that's different. Those *federales*, they're shooters man. They don't even ask questions afterwards. They just want someone to blame for the crime and usually it's the closest warm body. Guilt doesn't mean anything to those *pendejos*."

"Hey, I understand. If you don't want to be involved, it's okay. I don't like this either. I have no idea at all what's going on here. Antiay and I weren't married or anything. We didn't even live together and I guess, technically, we were even free to date others. That's the way we wanted it. But if I had been inclined to...uh...marry...it would have been her. In other words, I'm gonna find her killer and the reason why if it kills me."

"I'll help if I can. Where do you want me to start?"

"We better get to the *federales* before they come looking for us. It's always better that way. Keep them off guard. Can you call someone and tell them I'd like to make a statement?"

"Sure, no problem. I'll be back in a minute."

Freddy got up and went to call. I ordered some more coffee because he was wrong about one thing. He wasn't going to be back in a minute. That was a meaningless phrase in Mexico. Freddy had been hanging around too many *gringos*.

Freddy. You couldn't help but like the guy, and as long as you didn't have a beautiful, bored wife hanging around, you could trust him. Freddy was an ex-cop who did private investigative work in both of the Mexican States of Baja, California. He'd been with the Judicial Police of Baja, stationed in Tijuana, but he'd got caught in an affair with his superior officer's wife. Freddy resigned from the force and moved to La Paz where he started his own business chasing down unfaithful spouses and doing international liaison work for people like me. He has a very funny story about the time he was hired to discover the lover of an unfaithful wife, and it turned out to be himself. Small towns.

Anyway, I'd done business with him a few times using him to trace missing persons and things like that. I finally met him in person one day when he turned up in my office in Venice Beach, California. It seemed that Cupid had finally turned the tables on him and his current "true love" had run off to Los Angeles with someone who had promised her the bright lights of Hollywood. Yeah, well, I didn't tell him she was probably real popular right now down on the corner of Hollywood and Vine.

His *macho* couldn't admit he had it coming. He wanted me to help find her, but instead I introduced him to a couple of other aspiring actresses I knew. Three days later he was back in my office, hand-in-hand with one of them. He thanked me and said they were off to La Paz to be married. I don't know how long the affair lasted. Probably not long. They don't call him Fast Freddy for nothing.

I sipped my coffee and looked out at the *gringo* sailboats riding at anchor. At the peak of the season there could be up to two hundred boats riding the waves in La Paz Bay, and another hundred or so tied up in the various marinas. Of course the boats were as different as the people who owned and sailed them. Everything from leaky old wood schooners to the sleekest modern racing designs. From decrepit old anti-social sailors to alcoholic multi-millionaires, and vice-versa. The one thing they all had in common is that they liked to mess around in boats.

The sailors, or cruisers, as they call themselves to differentiate live-aboards from weekend sailors, communicate daily on VHF radio. At eight o'clock each morning they broadcast a Cruiser's Net on which they exchange everything from weather and recipes to crew members, including, often enough, lovers and spouses. Yeah well, the *gringo* community was definitely small town. I decided I'd check in as soon as possible with my friend, Hal Lewis. His boat, a thirty-foot tri-maran named "Harbor Hog," was tied up at the *Marina de la Paz*.

The *Marina de la Paz* is the largest and most centrally located of La Paz's marinas, so it's the hub of the gossip network. Hal might have picked up some information I could use, and if not I'd have him tune in to the drums. He was a funny guy, Hal was. He had a passion for overweight women, even though he himself was kind of skinny. Hal had a way of seeing things that other people missed. I'd have to check in with him.

"Rick!" Back from his errand, Freddy seated himself at the table. "Check this out. I got it in the *oficina*."

He tossed a copy of the local newspaper, *Diario Peninsular*, in front of me. Spread over half a page of the crime section was the dead blonde from last night. Okay, it was Antiay. Her mangled body anyway. Somehow, try as I might, I couldn't think of that mess on the bed in that cheap hotel as someone I knew. It wasn't. Antiay had been a live, beautiful, intelligent, sensuous woman. The photo was just so much buzzard meat.

I tried to read the caption under the photo, but couldn't translate the Spanish. I handed it back to Freddy.

"What's it say?"

"It says, more or less, that the body of a *gringa* woman was found in a hotel. The *policiá* suspect she committed suicide. They said a gun was found in her hand and they are investigating."

"Yeah, figures they'd call it a suicide. That way they can either bury it, or find so-called new evidence later. At least the heat's off me."

"Maybe not. The *Federale* on the phone said they are anxious to question you about the death of the *gringa* woman. Those were his very words—he said *nada* about suicide. He said for you to be there within an hour or they will come for you."

"I guess that makes it a date. Should I take flowers?"

Freddy shook his head and smiled. "It's up to you my friend. Do you want me to go with you to interpret or something?"

"No, I'm not going to make it easy for them. If they can't handle it, tough shit. I don't want to give them the idea you're my constant companion. Maybe they'll forget about you."

"*Bueno. Gracias*, Rick. I'll find out what I can about the big-money boat."

"Great. And if you could get a copy of the police report, that would be grand."

Freddy's eyebrows raised, then he stood up. "I should have ordered a more expensive breakfast. *Hasta luego.*"

"Later," I said, picking up the check. Freddy had expensive tastes, so I knew his help would cost me a lot more than a meal or two. He dreamed in U.S. dollars. There goes the vacation budget. It looked like I was going to have to get back to Los Angeles working for dollars myself, when this was finished. Like the prostitute says, "It doesn't pay to fall in love."

Chapter Four

WHEN I WALKED into the Federal Judicial Police Building, I wasn't in the best of moods. I felt the way you do when you lift a rock and encounter a nest of scorpions. You'd rather not have known they were there, but now that you do, you only want to squash them. There are a lot of wonderful things about Mexico, but like anywhere, there are a few things that are not so nice. The *federales* have a tradition of corruption, which has been inflamed by the drug wars.

Yeah, well that was their problem and they were about to have another one. I needed some anger to deal with these guys and all I had to do was think about Antiay, and the body on the bed and those two cops laughing....

I walked up to the emaciated scarecrow at the desk and introduced myself. "Hello, I'm Rick Sage. I have an appointment to make a statement about—"

Perhaps he didn't speak English, because he shot some rapid-fire Spanish back at me as he brushed away a real fly. So I tried it his way. "*Soy* Rick Sage. *Tengo...una cita...con...con...*"

Something registered in his tired brain this time, because I barely had my name out before he reached over and pressed the old-fashioned buzzer fastened to the rickety table.

The door behind him burst open and saved me the embarrassment of acknowledging I had reached a linguistic dead-end. The three plainclothes officers who were competing for first-place honors in the grab-the-gringo-and-frisk-him contest, didn't seem to be too concerned about the ritual of formal introduction in a cross-cultural milieu. They just grabbed me, searched me not-so-gently, and hustled me down the hall. Too bad because I've got my '*cómo está—bien—y usted—bien, gracias*' down pretty good.

I'd decided to go along for the ride, but when they pushed me down a flight of concrete stairs and one of them hollered "*¡Andale gringo cabrón!*" I lost my balance and my composure at the same time.

I feigned injury and hunched crumpled near the door at the bottom of the stairs for the half-instant it took them to reach me. They were having fun now and were once again competing to be first—this time for kick-the-*gringo* honors. Well, boys will be boys, but I was tired of playing the *piñata.* I grabbed the winner's foot and presented him his trophy—a quick twist that made a sharp "crack" sound as he screamed his acceptance speech.

Then the four of us were tumbling through the door in a whirlwind of feet, arms, legs, and heads that must have looked like some multi-appendaged alien creature at war with itself. This was starting to be fun, so I poked another eye and took an elbow in the nose. All it needed was one of those discordant *Sinaloa* bands for accompaniment.

Then the door across the hall slammed open and a commanding voice tried to calm the raging beast. "*¡Alto! ¡Alto! ¡Basta!*"

And for my benefit, in English, "Stop! Enough! Mr. Sage is our guest. Please, Mr. Sage, come in and have a seat." He motioned to a chair as my playmates disentangled themselves amid much grumbling and groaning.

Getting to my feet I managed one last elbow to the nearest gut and was rewarded by a gushing expletive in Spanish that threatened to restart the brawl.

"*¡Basta!* Please Mr. Sage. Come in. Have a seat."

I decided to observe the truce for now so I could find out what they had in mind. Back in the stairwell I'd stopped worrying about any consequences, so if they wanted to play some more, well, war is hell. In men, the need for revenge is sometimes stronger than the instinct for survival. Don't ask me why.

I sat down and looked around the room while I tried to stop the bleeding from my nose. Blood was getting all over my shirt. The room was one of the confessionals I'd heard about. When the *federales* arrested you, they brought you here to see "the priest" with his torture tools. Shocks to the gonads—that kind of thing. The devices were probably in those drawers over against the end wall. When the pain of your sins became too much for you, you confessed. The Inquisition had nothing on these boys.

The room was sparsely furnished with just my plain wooden chair and another behind the table in front of the drawers. The only interesting thing in the room was the six-foot by four-foot two-way glass in the wall over the torture-tool drawers.

I thought of Antiay as my playmate and his wounded friends limped out of the room and were replaced by a fresh tag-team of four gorillas who made television's pro wrestlers look like computer techies. It seemed we were ready to begin, which was good. I had a lot more anger to work out and there was no one else I'd rather take it out on, at the moment. Two of these guys had stood laughing over Antiay's dead body, and I felt very bad I'd let them get away with it. I began to wonder just who might be behind that glass watching the show. I stared at the guy who thought he was in charge. Despite his commanding voice, he was a bit on the thin side. But you could tell he was used to being in charge. Well, maybe, if he was careful and polite.

He stared back at me. "Mr. Sage, my name is Captain Rodriguez. I need to question you about the *gringa* who died last night. We have reason to believe she was involved in the drug trade. Do you have any knowledge of this?"

So they weren't interested in the murder after all. I stared past Captain Rod at the two-way glass. It was really starting to bug me—who was back there? They were trying to push some drug angle, but why?

"The woman you're referring to had nothing to do with drugs as far as I know," I replied. "Why don't you get off your ass and find out who murdered her?"

That put some fire in his eyes and washed away a bit of the smooth facade.

"We have dealt with *machos* before, *cabrón*. I would advise you to cooperate." His eyes shifted to the drawers for an instant. He probably couldn't wait to get started. "Your *gringa* whore isn't worth our time. We would thank the person for ridding us of such trash. You will—"

I was on him before he knew it, grabbing his throat and balls and lifting him high over my head. The glass of the two-way window shattered as his body flew through it. Amongst falling shards of glass I saw for an instant the shocked face of Bill White, the DEA honcho, just before the wooden chair crashed down on my head and shoulders and sprawled me on the floor. Barely on the edge of consciousness I heard the voice of White. "Don't kill him. We have ways of dealing with Mr. Rick Sage. Just get him out of here."

I forced open my eyes but wished I hadn't because all I saw before I blacked out was the steel-toed boot coming at my face.

I WOKE UP in a warm rain. Even through my broken nose, I smelled a horrible stench. I heard an old-geezer voice croak, "Like your shower pal?"

It took much effort, but one eye finally opened just in time to see someone fly over me, knocking the derelict backward with his pecker still in his hand.

"Uhhh! Shit...hy'd you do that?"

"I told you before, dude," another voice answered, "I'm tired of your sloppy ass. It's bad enough in here without you pissing all over the floor."

I could see now that I was lying near a filthy commode, but I still couldn't move. Maybe I was dreaming. A nightmare, a very realistic one. I sure hoped so.

I felt arms lift me up. They dragged me across the floor and heaved me against the wall. That hurt.

"There dude." It was the voice of the guy who had just tossed the derelict. "That wiped-out old alky doesn't even know where he is. The *Mexicanos* in here are about ready to do him in and he don't even know it. Man, that must've been some wave you took. You're a mess—better clean you up a bit. I'll get my towel. Don't go away."

The kid had a sense of humor. I watched him make his way to a sink, then I rested my eye. Funny how everything is relative. The surfer kid seemed like an angel in these surroundings. A big, tan, nineteen-year-old kid who probably believed life began and ended where the sand meets the sea. Well, I guess you couldn't get more innocent than that.

I felt the cool wetness of the towel and thought I'd never known anything finer. *I owe you kid. I can guess why you're in here, but I'm gonna do everything I can to get you out...Whoa boy...I don't know if I can get myself out. I don't even know where I am.*

"Where are we?"

"We're in the slammer. Don't you remember? Guess not—you really tied one on. That must have been some bar fight. Hope the other dude looks this bad. I took a header into a gravel shoal one time and didn't look as bad as you. There. About the best I can do. Wish I could offer you a doobie—hell, wish I could offer myself one. They say you can get stuff in here if you've got money—'course I got nothing. Another boardhead gettin' out gave me this stuff or I wouldn't even have a blanket. Hey, they don't give you nothing but the cold floor in here man..."

His hyper-speed rap reached a dead-end and he slumped down against the wall beside me. I glanced around our cell. It was fifteen square feet with about the same number of bodies sprawled in various positions over most of the available space. A tiny corner of hell for sure.

"How'd you get in here kid?" I moaned through cracked lips. "Pot?"

"How'd you guess?" he sighed. "Mary Wanna-be for sure. Guess it shows, huh? Yeah, jeez. Guess I was set up. Been down by Del Cabo for the Spring curve—nice swells—ran outta smoke and a friend tells me *Mazatlán's* the place. Gave me a name, so I parked the Dub downtown and took the Baja Express over—that fast catamaran ferry they got running from here now. I get there and call the dude up. Met me in a hotel room—Mexican dude—but got pissed as hell man 'cause I only wanted a few ounces. Said he dealt in quantity so I agreed to take a kilo—told him I just wanted to try it—tried to mellow him out, you know. I lied and said my parents were rich and I could get money for more, if everything was cool. He went big time for that—said he had a connection in La Paz could get me all the coke I wanted, strictly quantity though. I said yeah, maybe. We partied awhile—he was real interested in surfing—then I took the kilo and caught the Express back over. I know it was a set-up 'cause the *federales* were waiting for me at the dock back here in La Paz—shoulda known—all that crap he told me about being the son of the governor and having a rich German girlfriend on some million-dollar yacht...shoulda read the curl quicker man, you know..."

Yeah I knew all right, like a kick in the face. A German girlfriend on a million-dollar yacht, and the governor's son? Was it another coincidence? All the hurt in my body suddenly faded. There was no pain like the big lie. Did I really want to know more? I was sure I didn't. Damn you Antiay! And damn me, too, but it wasn't in my nature to quit. Still, it made sense that the first answers in this case came from a room in hell.

I forced myself to crawl up the wall until I stood upright. Then, on my own two feet. Yeah well, nothing was broken, except maybe my nose again.

"You okay?"

"No."

"You don't look like no alky dude. What you doing here? Catch the wrong wave?"

"Yeah, something like that. A murder wave. My parents were murdered when I was four...I found their bodies...my earliest memory. The cops never did figure out who did it. Maybe that's what got me here. I dunno...shit. Maybe it was my older brother getting himself killed in Vietnam. Damn dead heroes...someone keeps killing off everyone I care about...and I just keep chasing them."

"Jeez, that's harsh dude. That's really harsh. You got a hard ride."

"Huh?"

"I mean I'm sorry 'bout your bro. That Vietnam thing was pretty weird I guess."

"Yeah, I guess." I hadn't even realized I was talking out loud. My head was really throbbing. I put my hand on it to try to hold it together. I must've really taken a wallop.

"How long I been in here kid?"

"They brought you in last night, sometime. I figure it's about noon now—gettin' so I can tell time by my stomach. Wish they had a window in here though."

That made it going on twenty-four hours since I'd seen Freddy. I was thinking he should have found me by now, when a door clanged and a guard showed at the bars. He opened the door and pointed his club at me. "*¡Andale!*," he said, and it was *déjà vu* all over again.

"Okay, thanks kid," I said, shaking his hand. "And don't worry. I'll get you out of here somehow."

"Yeah, sure Dude," he answered cynically. It's always sad to see the loss of innocence.

As I hobbled through the door the guard growled, "*¡Más rápido, pendejo!*" and raised his stick to strike. I gathered all my remaining strength, fueled it with the total disgust and hatred I felt for the world at this moment, and focused it through my one good eye, burning a challenge at the cowardly guard.

"*Con permiso*," I spat at him, and he wilted, the stick dropping to his side, his gaze averted.

"*Pasale*," he whispered back. "*Por favor.*"

Chapter Five

OUT OF SHEER stubbornness, that animal quality some people mistake for courage, I refused Freddy's assistance until we were out of the building and safely in the parking lot, where I crumpled onto the hood of his Camaro. Freddy hadn't said a word since the "*¡Ay, Dios mio!*" he'd whispered when they turned me over to him. Even now, as he opened the car door and helped me onto the leather upholstery, his string of curses seemed to suggest unnatural acts performed between consenting *federales* and their herd of goats. Even though my command of Spanish isn't that good, I didn't hear anything I couldn't agree with.

"*¡Dios mio!*" he said again as he started the car and turned on the air conditioning. "You smell like a goat in season who has been drinking cheap *tequila.* What happened to you my friend? You need a doctor very bad. Your eye will need stitches I think. That is a very bad cut. They said they found you drunk on the street—that you must have been in a fight in a *cantina.*"

"Freddy, I'm afraid this is just the beginning. They want to make me look bad so it will be easier to do what they want to later."

"Yes, it is an old trick. Now that you've been arrested for public drunkenness no one will believe your story. I think you should forget about her now. Just go home to Los Angeles. After I get you to a doctor of course. Where do you wish to go?"

"I need to lay low for a couple of days. Somewhere no one would look for me. They might just want to finish me off while I'm down. Do you know my friend Dr. Acosta? Where he lives?"

"Pepe? Sure, I know the place, but he's a—"

"Yeah, well it's the last place anybody would look don't you think?"

"Yeah, but you need—"

"It's okay, Freddy. He and his wife are good friends of mine. They'll take care of me. If I'm not mistaken, there is more than one party who wants me out of the way, but I don't think they agree on tactics."

Freddy was weaving through traffic now, driving faster than I thought the situation called for. He was usually a careful driver. He didn't want a scratch on his new car. Something must have scared him.

"Careful," I said as I reached up and twisted the rear view mirror toward me. "You're gonna get us—Jesus! I look like hell."

"Yeah, it's bad all right," Freddy replied. "Just lay back there until I get you to Pepe's."

I did like he said. The face in the mirror looked like the mask of a dead man. And if I wasn't more careful, that's exactly what it would be.

I LET THE hot water run over me as I leaned against the wall. I had to lock my knees to keep my legs from collapsing under me and the blood was starting to flow again as the dirt washed away from the cut over my right eyebrow. It seemed nothing had ever felt so good as this hot shower did, and the blood flow would help clean the cut. Pepe's clinic was attached to his house by a patio, and when Freddy had helped me into the clinic, Pepe crossed himself and said, "That must have been one bad bull. Let's get him into the house."

Lourdes, his wife, met us halfway there and suddenly I was engulfed in a whirlwind of attention the President himself would envy. Lourdes was one of those women for whom the word 'mother' was created.

"He needs to be cleaned up first," she said. "Can you stand up to take a shower?" she asked, not waiting for a reply, "I'm sorry we don't have a tub, but Pepe you help him, and Freddy, you, too. I'll get the bandages and turn down the bed."

When I finally shut off the water and opened the door, I felt much better, if slightly woozy, and all of the attention was starting to embarrass me. I tried to protest as Freddy and Pepe wrapped towels around me and helped me into the bedroom, but then I almost fell, landing on the bed.

"Maybe I need help after all," I said. Pepe leaned over and looked at my eye as I lay back on the pillow.

"You need stitches to close this cut. I'll call a doctor."

"You're a doctor," I said. "You do it."

"I'm a veterinarian. I'm afraid being bullheaded doesn't qualify you to be one of my patients."

"Pepe, you've stitched a thousand wounds and more. The human ego is the only thing that makes my flesh different from theirs. Besides, it could be much more dangerous for me to see a doctor right now. Just consider it an emergency. Besides...sorry, I'm very tired and...need to sleep..."

I AWOKE TO the early morning sounds of birds, with sunlight streaming through the window. I felt over my eye and there were bandages. *Good work, Doc.* I'd seen Pepe operate on a friend's dog—that's how we'd met. The mutt had been torn up by a larger dog and Pepe had sewn him up finer than a plastic surgeon could have. In fact, Pepe would have made a fine surgeon except that he grew up on a dairy farm near *Tijuana* and he liked animals better. Sometimes I had to agree with him.

I lay there in bed for a while thinking about what had happened the last couple of days. For the past year La Paz had been a wonderful refuge for me and I had begun to feel like my old self, maybe better, until Antiay was murdered.

I had never met as many nice people as I had here in Mexico. For the most part, the Mexican people were warm and open-hearted. They were very family-oriented and they made strangers feel a part of that family. Even with a language barrier, if you tried to communicate, they would respond.

That's what made me so angry about the last two days. It just wasn't La Paz. Somebody was messing up a nice town and I was starting to take that almost as personally as if they had sworn at my mother. People like Pepe and Lourdes and their three kids didn't deserve to have L.A.-type crime invade their neighborhood. They were the type of people who were always helping others at the same time they were both working extra jobs just to make ends meet. Damn.

I got out of bed and went into the bathroom. My clothes had been laid out on the dresser next to the bed. And in the bathroom I found my shaving kit. Someone had gone to my place for supplies.

I looked in the mirror. It wasn't a pretty sight. Black and blue and swollen. But I was still functional at least. Except for my nose, I had no broken bones—maybe a cracked rib or two but I could work with that. And damn, I chuckled to myself, it was worth it to have seen the look on White's face. I'd forgotten that. Hell, I felt better already.

I shaved carefully, did my other bathroom chores, and got dressed. I was putting on my socks when someone knocked at the door.

"Yeah, come in."

It was Pepe. "*Buenos dias*, Rick. How are you feeling?"

"I feel like a new man thanks to you."

"You look like a new man. Well, different anyway. You are lucky nothing much was broken. A couple more days and you will be able to ride again."

Pepe had once been the Mexican National Champion Bull Rider. He had had most of his bones broken at one time or another, but had been forced to stop riding when a one-ton bull did a hat dance on his spine. The doctor told him he was very lucky, but if he rode again he risked permanent paralysis. After he recovered, he rode one more time just to prove to himself he hadn't lost his nerve, then he retired. At five-foot-four, Pepe was, pound for pound, the toughest guy I knew. And he didn't have a mean bone in his body.

"I think I'll take a break from riding those *hombres* for a day or two. I feel like I've been danced on by a whole herd of your bulls. It sure was fun though."

"*Federales?*"

"Yeah. Freddy fill you in?"

"We read about Antiay. Freddy said the *federales* are covering up for her murderer and that you...ah...had a talk with them about it. By the way, I picked up your motorcycle for you—and Lourdes has breakfast ready. If you want, you can tell me more while we eat."

"Sounds great. I haven't eaten for two days. Lourdes' cooking— *mmmm*—what a way to end a fast."

"Wait 'til you see it. She's got enough food going down there to feed an army, or you and me."

"Let's have at it, pardner."

Two plates of *chilaquiles* with chicken, four fried eggs, six pancakes, half a pound of bacon, several *tortillas* (two with honey), three glasses of fresh squeezed orange juice, two helpings of refried beans, two pieces of homemade flan and a couple cups of coffee later, I really did feel like a new man. From a bird's eye view, my stomach looked like twice the man I had been.

"ONE MORE PIECE of flan, Rick? We need to eat it up."

"No thanks, Lourdes. That would be the piece that broke the camel's hump."

Both Lourdes and Pepe grew up near the border and speak fluent English. Parts of their families are citizens of the United States. But they didn't always get the strange humor of the north. And sometimes nobody got mine. Lourdes just smiled. She did understand that I was full. After all she'd prepared the feast.

"Here's some more coffee. You two go out on the patio while I get this cleaned up."

We grabbed our newly-filled cups, and for once Pepe and I both did as we were told.

"Pepe, I have another favor to ask of you."

"What is it Rick? I will be glad to help if I can."

We were sitting under the grape vines with bunches of unripe grapes glowing in the leaf-filtered light of the morning sun. I was embarrassed to ask for another favor.

"You told me once, I think, that you had a friend in the Prosecutor's office."

"Yes. Sure. He is the chief prosecutor, which means, in our system, he's in charge of the judges and the police. But if you were just charged with public drunkenness and you are out of jail now—that means the whole thing is over. They let you go."

"No, it's not me, Pepe. When I was in the cell, I met a young kid who'd been busted for drugs. He helped me out. I'm sure he was set up by some of the same people who might be involved in Antiay's murder. He's not entirely innocent, but I'm afraid if I leave him in there and I act on his information, someone may figure it out. If so, his life would be endangered. Besides, like I said, he helped me out."

"I understand Rick. Trouble is, anything with drugs and *gringos* is bad news. Your government is so self-righteous when it comes to the drug question that our people love the opportunity to show that you are the cause. Our problem is the effect. How much did he get caught with?"

"One kilo of *marijuana*."

"No cocaine?"

"No. At least that's what he told me. I believe him though. This kid's not much of a liar. He tells you his life history in the first ten minutes. And that's all it takes. I'd say he's still a pretty innocent, honest kid—all things considered. If he stays much longer in that hell-hole though, he won't be for long."

"*Marijuana* is an old drug in this country. It never caused much problem before, so people don't get too excited about it. Now cocaine— that's another story. Of course I wouldn't want my kids involved with any of it. Even alcohol. But what can you do? The kids just don't realize what they're getting into sometimes."

"Yeah, you're right. I've got a feeling this kid may have wised up a whole bunch already. But it won't do him any good if he doesn't get another chance."

"I'll do what I can Rick. My friend and I grew up together and did a few crazy things when we were young—like everyone. Nothing like these kids today...still I think he'll listen. And I just happen to have saved his favorite brood mare's life last week. I think he'd give me his first-born child right now if I asked for it."

"I don't know the surfer kid's name."

"Oh, that's no problem. It's still a small town even if it is changing. I hope your experiences of the last few days haven't soured you on La Paz, Rick. Sure the *federales* are bad, but even the Federal Government is trying to get the corruption under control. Here in La Paz, the majority of people are good honest citizens. My friend the prosecutor is an honest man and so are most of the people I know. It's an embarrassment to me that you should have met the few dishonest ones."

"Pepe, I haven't met any finer people than I've found in La Paz. I already feel like you and Lourdes are family. I was just thinking earlier that that's what makes me so mad about what's been happening. I wish La Paz could stay a peaceful place a while longer."

"Yes, let's hope so. I better get going and see what I can do about your young friend."

"Okay, I'll take these cups in to Lourdes."

When I walked into the kitchen, Lourdes was just putting the first of the dishes into a sink full of hot soapy water.

"That's what I need to soak my sore hands in," I said as I bumped her out of the way.

"Oh, no, Rick, you go rest now. I can take care of the dishes. Pepe would kill me if he knew I let you do that."

"Then we won't tell him. Besides, I think I'm the one he would kill for giving you ideas."

"Oh, no, Pepe works very hard. But the last thing I'd want would be him busting up my dishes trying to help. He has a lot more in common with those bulls he used to ride than you think."

By this time I was well-established in the soapy dishes department and needed all of my concentration to keep from breaking them myself.

"Since you insist, Rick. Thanks. But it's our secret."

"That's a promise."

Five minutes later, the doorbell rang and I heard Lourdes let someone in.

"Rick's in the kitchen...ah...just a minute, Freddy, I'll get him for—"

"That's all right, Lourdes. I just have to give him this. Rick, here's the report you—well, I'll be damned..."

I hadn't had time to get off the apron that Lourdes had tied around my waist, and soap suds dripped from my hands. Before I knew it, Freddy was doubled up with laughter. Yeah well....

I finished the dishes while Freddy composed himself. He was still chuckling as we made our way out to the patio for yet another cup of coffee from Lourdes' bottomless pot.

"Freddy, even though I have a maid, this is not the first time I've ever done the dishes."

"Sure Rick (chuckle, chuckle), but I was thinking how bad you looked yesterday, only...my friend...when I saw you, you looked so...different (chuckle, chuckle). I thought...maybe his brain is damaged...he thinks he is a woman now..." He broke up into laughter once again.

I took the manila envelope he'd dropped on the table and opened it. Inside was a copy of the police report on Antiay's death. There were no pictures, but I didn't need them anyway. The scene was branded onto my memory. The report was only significant in what it left out. And they were sloppy. They said she had used a .32 caliber revolver to kill herself. Any idiot could see from the amount of damage to the head that a large caliber weapon had been used, like a .44 magnum, or a .45. Well that was good. If I needed to call for an inquiry, it was nice to have some obvious discrepancies.

Yeah, they were covering up all right. Which meant that both the murderer and the police knew a lot more about this than I did. Unless of course, they were one and the same. Not a comforting thought. It wouldn't be easy for a *gringo* Private Detective to convict the Mexican Federal Judicial Police of a felony crime that didn't exist on record. Pablo's burro would be a better bet to win the Kentucky Derby.

Opening the envelope had sobered Freddy and I felt his intent gaze as I stuffed the report back into it. "Thanks."

"It's nothing my friend. But perhaps they are right. Maybe she did...you know. Maybe it is better if you go home now. She is dead anyway. There is nothing you can do except cause more trouble for yourself."

I looked at him. That was the second time he'd suggested I leave. And only an idiot would seriously believe this had been suicide. Didn't he know me? Didn't he understand?

"The only way anybody is going to get me out of here before I get Antiay's murderer, is if they get me first—understand my friend?"

"Sure Rick, okay. Okay. Take it easy."

I realized suddenly that I had grabbed Freddy's shirt and had dragged him halfway across the table spilling his coffee cup and rattling mine. I released him, embarrassed.

"I was just worried about you," Freddy said, straightening his shirt.

"Yeah, okay. I'm sorry Freddy. I thought I had it under control and then reading this damn report I guess...you've been a big help and I'm really sorry."

"Hey, it's okay man. *No problema.* I understand. It's just a shirt, man. I'll send you the bill." He laughed and I smiled.

"Thanks pal. You do that."

"It's nothing. Hey, I almost forgot. That big yacht? It's owned by some rich German guy named Jurgen Grossman. I guess he's even on board now. I found that out from the Port Captain's office."

Lourdes had spotted the spilled coffee and was bustling around now cleaning it up.

"I'll get it Lourdes. It was my fault," I protested.

"It's no problem," she replied. "You did the dishes, I'll get this." Obviously she wasn't going to be happy until she had paid me back ten times for those few dishes I'd washed. Might as well accept it and let her go ahead. Freddy went on with his story.

"But then I tried to talk to one of the crew when he came into the municipal dock. I pretended I was a Captain of the ferry to *Topolobampo* and said it was an interesting boat he had. He was Latino, maybe Colombian, but *¡Ay yi!* he was very unfriendly. He only wanted to discuss my ancestors, and suggested I might join them. Then I mentioned his, and it would have been a very nice fight except someone pulled him away. Too bad—he was such a nice *cabrón*."

We both laughed at that.

"Be careful, Freddy. Some of these guys don't play by the rules, and you have such a pretty face.

"Ah, but I would hope not to win my fights so badly as you, my friend."

"Yeah, well, I'll try to keep that in mind next time."

I told him about my encounter with White, and the interrogator asking about Antiay and drugs. "Did you hear anything about the DEA? Why they're in town?"

"*No, nada mucho.* Maybe it's just a meeting. There doesn't seem to be a big drug bust about to happen or my friend would know. This *hombre*, White, is staying at the *Gran Baja* Hotel though."

Lourdes brought new coffee cups and refilled them. She also brought some cookies in the shape of little pigs, which is exactly what I felt like. I couldn't have eaten one of their tails, but I didn't tell her that. "Thanks, Lourdes."

"*Gracias*," Freddy mumbled as he bit off half a pig.

"I just can't figure the drug angle," I said as Lourdes disappeared into the house. "I would have sworn Antiay wasn't involved in any way, but..." and I told him about my encounter with the surfer in the cell, and his story about the Victor, the governor's son.

"Pepe's trying to help get the kid out of jail. If we can, and I can get him on a plane out of Mexico, then my next move will be to go to Mazatlán and look up my old friend, the governor's son. I don't dare do anything, though, until I'm sure the surfer is safe. If anybody gets word of it, the kid will never get out of that cell alive."

"What a mess, Rick. Now the governor yet. *Ay!*"

"Yeah, it gets weirder and weirder."

"Is there anything you want me to do? You want me to go to Mazatlán?"

"No, I don't want you any more involved than you already are. Somebody is playing this one for keeps, maybe several people. I appreciate the offer but I promised I'd keep you out of it if there are drugs involved, and it's beginning to look more and more like there are. It's best if you just lay low and keep your eyes and ears open for me. Okay?"

"Okay, whatever you say my friend. I do have a couple of things of my own that I've been neglecting."

"They wouldn't be female kinds of things would they?"

"Let's just say, they're the kinds of things that suspect you of doing other things if you don't show up for a couple of days—"

"Or nights," I finished for him. "Yeah well, we don't need anyone else mad at us. It'd be terrible to get through this mess and get shot by a disgruntled girlfriend."

"You said it my friend. Don't even mention that."

We stood up as Freddy prepared to leave.

"Okay, thanks again Freddy."

"*De nada.*"

Pepe walked in.

"*Buenos días* Freddy. *Hola* Rick. Good news. They're going to let your young friend out, but we have to get him on a plane tonight—"

"*Perdón*, but I must go. *Bueno Suerte*, Rick. *Hasta Luego*, Pepe," Freddy said as he continued out the door.

"*Hasta Luego* Freddy," Pepe said, and waved.

"Later," I said. And then to Pepe, "Hey, that's great. You did it."

"Yes. I walked in to my friend and I said, remember that time... And he interrupted me—he knows me well—and he said, what is it this time Pepe? I know every time you start to talk about old times like that it costs me a very big favor. So I told him everything, even about Antiay, and he got very angry. He said, someone is messing up our beautiful home, Pepe. I've never seen him so angry. He said he knows something big is going on but he doesn't know what it is, so it must be illegal because they know he is honest. He said he is sorry about the death of your girlfriend but there is nothing he can do about that. It's a Federal matter now.

"I told him we understood that. It is only that you are afraid the boy will be harmed. He said he understood about the entrapment. They have been getting a lot of cases like that lately. It is because of the American pressure to show some results in the drug war. If they catch enough small fish, and there are always lots of small fish, he said, then they can let the big fish get away."

"Yeah, just like war, Pepe," I said. "The little guys get killed and the Generals go on to start another one."

"Isn't it always so?" Pepe replied, shaking his head. "Anyway, my friend said it would be no problem to release the kid if we can get him on a plane to California. I said fine, and he called the airline himself and reserved a seat, under police orders, for the 7:10 flight to Los Angeles, tonight. Two officers will deliver him to the airport and see that he gets on the plane. You can be there if you like."

"Yeah, I think I'll do that."

"The only thing is, he has to forfeit all of his belongings except what he is wearing. My friend said it would attract too much attention to try to get his stuff back. Just consider it a fine, he said."

"I don't think the kid is going to argue that point. In fact, I know he isn't. He doesn't expect to see daylight for the next twenty years."

"And he probably wouldn't if it wasn't for you."

"And a lot of help from some friends. Thanks again, Pepe. I don't know how to thank your friend."

"He doesn't want any thanks. He hoped you would be able to get to the bottom of this mess somehow and he wished you luck. He said the only chance was for someone outside the system, like you, to raise so much trouble that the political types would have to back away from whatever is going on. Lift the rock and watch them scurry, is the way he put it."

"Yeah, well, I guess this town has to grow up sometime, but maybe it can at least grow up honest."

"Let's hope so. That was the other thing my friend said. He said there is a strong rumor around town that some powerful people are trying to bring Las Vegas casino-style gambling into La Paz. He said it's just a rumor but something like that could be behind whatever is going on. Or it could be just drugs. What do you think, Rick?"

"Damn! I don't know. Every time I turn around, there's another snake raising its head. Maybe this town isn't as innocent as we wish it was."

Chapter Six

IT TOOK ME a minute to realize I had been dreaming. I looked at my watch. 5:10 p.m. Jeez, I'd slept for more than five hours. What a dream. It was one of those that keep changing, and already I couldn't remember parts of it. Antiay and I had been registering at a hotel, like we were on a honeymoon. But then she started dissolving, only the desk clerk didn't seem to notice, and then she was some kind of cheap hooker and the clerk called the house detective over and he turned out to be Bill White. He kept saying we don't allow that type in here, and then all of sudden it was some German hotel in 1940 and you could hear machine guns outside and White was an SS Agent pulling on Antiay's arm saying he recognized her—the bitch. There were soldiers all around us trying to arrest her and I was screaming, "That isn't her. That isn't her." I opened my eyes still trying to find a way to save her. The sound of gunfire turned out to be the click-click-click the ceiling fan made as it went around and around.

Damn! I was sorry I'd gone back to bed, but Lourdes had insisted, and my head had been thumping like an oversized parade drum. So I took the pills she gave me, just before I'd called my friend, the Old Prof up at Riverside. After that call I'd wanted to sleep, thinking I couldn't handle one more complication or my head really would split like a too tight drumhead. But what he'd told me had kept going around and around in my mind. I guess the pills finally took hold though, because now it was five hours of bad dreams later.

I thought about Fred Metcalf again. We called him the Old Prof because that was his handle on the Ham radio nets he had communicated with for years. The handle had carried over to the computer networks he was involved in. Fred was, in reality, Dr. Metcalf, Professor of Mathematics at the University of California, Riverside. That was in his second life. Before that he had been with the CIA for twenty years specializing in Eastern Europe—I suppose trying to encourage the defection or employment of scientific types. He never talked about it much but what he had said made it all seem scholarly and quite removed from the James Bond school of cloak and dagger. In the end he'd become disillusioned though, so he took his early twenty-year retirement and went back to his first loves—teaching and mathematics. He's retired now.

I knew he screened his telephone calls, which was odd considering his extensive involvement in communication via hams and computers. But his motto was "don't call us, we'll call you," and I couldn't fault him for that.

"Hello. Old Prof here. Leave a message."

"Hi Fred. This is Rick calling from Mexico."

I heard the jostle of a receiver being picked up, then his voice, "How are you, Rick? I was just thinking of you today. That I should call you and we'd get in some sailing. Haven't heard from you for a while. You detecting down in Mexico these days?"

"Aw, you guessed. Got a problem right up your alley and wonder if you can help me out."

"Be glad to, if I can."

"I need some information on a guy named Jurgen Grossman. German."

"That's easy. Jurgen Grossman was the name of a whiz-kid in East German intelligence back when I was hanging out in certain circles. He was the Stasi's man in charge of weapons distribution. He handled sales to other countries and terrorist groups. What else do you need to know?"

Just what I needed, another kick in the head. Damn it Antiay. I tried to sound cool. "Could be the guy. Can you find out what he's up to now? He's down here in La Paz living the good life on a very expensive yacht—definitely not government salary stuff."

"I'll do what I can. This guy was not above taking a cut off the top. What's this all about?"

"I can't go into detail. I don't know much right now. A friend of mine was murdered and this guy, Grossman, may have been involved. Maybe not. You know how it goes."

"Do you have a number I can reach you at? It's going to take a few hours. Maybe even tomorrow."

"I'm busy and don't know where I'll be so I better call you back if that's okay?"

"Sure, and don't worry about the time. This sounds important. Be careful down there. I'd hate to lose my favorite sailing partner."

"It ain't been all counting coconuts like I expected, but I imagine I'll still be around for that next Channel Islands cruise. Talk to you later, and thanks a lot." Then I hung up and took that five hour nap.

I rubbed my eyes. I was still groggy from the pills, and that didn't help when it came to trying to make sense out of this case. It was getting complicated—Mexico, drugs, ex-spies, the Las Vegas mob. Who'd believe it? I wished this case was simple—something nice and straightforward like a good old-fashioned love triangle. The kind where just before I wrestle the gun away from the murderer, she confesses. "Yeah I shot the bastard. Sure. He was a bum. I'm only sorry he died so easy." That kind of thing.

But no, I gotta be involved in this mess—where the only logical suspect is me. It was like quicksand. I kept sinking deeper and deeper but not getting any closer to where I wanted to go. For all the strange information I'd been picking up, none of it appeared to tie in to Antiay's death. The only real clue was the *federales* showing up at the murder scene ready to arrest someone. Some clue—cops at the scene of a murder.

I went into the bathroom and splashed some water on my face. Negative thinking was getting me nowhere. I wanted to get the murder scene out of my head, but something kept bringing it back—something that bothered me. *How about someone you loved lying there with her face blown off? That wasn't enough to bother you Mr. Tough Detective?*

Yeah, well, later then. I took a shower, then fired up the hog and headed to the airport.

I arrived at ten to seven. Since the surfer and his police escort hadn't arrived yet, I took the time to make a reservation for the morning flight to Mazatlán. I'd just finished when the squad car pulled up. It always made my day to see the police driving around in those Volkswagen Beetles. Almost as funny as a private eye on a motorcycle.

"How you doing kid?"

"So it was you? Thanks, Dude. I didn't believe you when you—"

"Yeah well, next time have more faith. Listen, we don't have much time." The officers were already making motions like we should break up this reunion. "The deal is, you leave all your stuff here, okay?"

"Jeez, I hate to lose that board, but yeah, sure, I never expected to see it again anyway."

The officers grabbed his arms and started to pull him toward the boarding gate. I trailed along.

"What's your name anyway?" I said.

"Aaron."

"Aaron. Any chance you remember the guy's phone number in Mazatlan?"

"Yeah sure, I memorized it because I'm always losing stuff I write down. But I got a good memory—" They were pushing him through the metal detector now. It went off on the cops, but no one bothered them about it.

He twisted around and hollered back at me. "It's seven-zero-four-zero-three."

"Seven-zero-four-zero-three. Thanks Aaron. And try to stay out of trouble will ya?"

"Yeah and thanks—thanks a million—hey I didn't get your name
dude, I wanna—"

But he was out the door onto the flight ramp. I didn't try to answer,
and headed for the parking lot. If nothing else came of this case, at least
the kid got his second chance. I hoped he made better use of it than the
guy I was flying to Mazatlán to see tomorrow. I sure as hell hoped so.
Victor, the governor's son, was going to have to answer some hard
questions in the morning. He owed me his freedom and I was going to
have to make him pay me back with some hard answers. What he was
doing to guys like Aaron was the same type of thing I'd kept from
happening to him a few years ago. Now he was old enough to know better.
Some guys just never learn.

I fired up the Hog and headed toward the highway out of town. It
rumbled beneath me like it knew what was coming, and liked it. I had a
couple of hours before Hal Lewis would show up at *La Terraza* restaurant
for his late evening meal. By then I might be hungry myself. Anyway I
wanted to see if he had heard anything of interest. He usually didn't get
there until around ten. In the meantime there was a full moon, and there is
nothing better for blowing cobwebs off the mind than a ride around the
Bay rumbling through the glow of silver moonbeams. Behind me on the
seat, like some old favorite blues number, rode the still warm memory of
Antiay. I couldn't help the tears, again.

I WAS IN A mellow mood by the time I parked at the *La Terraza*. Hal
wasn't there yet so I claimed a booth where I could watch the boats in the
bay riding at anchor, including one boat in particular. I ordered a Cuba
Libre and waited, enjoying the scenery.

La Terraza is an open-air restaurant just across the street from the
beach, and you can see all the way to the Mogote. It's one of those
wonderful places you find sometimes, not too frequently, where you
expect to see Bogart or Hemmingway walk in and sit down next to you. It
doesn't happen. Of course not—they're both long-dead. But their
characters usually show up. Those shadowy figures of imagination slip in
and out with a familiar nod to Hector, the *maitre'd* and owner. As the
overhead fans swirl the heavy air, the fat man, the brown-eyed beauty with
the mysterious smile, and the tough expatriate American with a hint of a
grin on weather-beaten lips, whisper together for a moment and drift on
their separate ways. I kid you not.

"Hello, Rick."

I looked up and there was Hal. "*Hola* Hal, I've been waiting for you.

Have a seat."

"Thanks. Some beautiful night, huh?"

"Yeah, sure is."

The waiter came by and we ordered.

"Sorry about Antiay, Rick. It's hard to believe she took her own life."

"She didn't. She was murdered."

"Wow! I knew suicide didn't sound like her. That's tough. She was a wonderful person. Does her death have any connection to the way your face looks? I've seen road-kill in better shape."

"Guess I got in the way of the official cover-up. They're determined to label her death a suicide, and so far they've done a good job of it. I don't even know if the cover-up has anything to do with the murder."

"Damn Rick, be careful. You cross the wrong crowd...they don't mess around down here."

"I intend to find Antiay's murderer."

"Okay, okay. Scares the heck out of me though."

"You heard anything on the grapevine about something unusual happening in La Paz? Like with the DEA or anything?"

"Drugs? You think...No, I haven't heard anything like that."

"What do you know about the big yacht in town?"

"That one out there?"

He pointed in the general direction of the only boat that could be called a big yacht. It dwarfed the other private boats riding at anchor in the moonlight.

"The *Southern Cross?* I heard some German guy owns it. Supposedly he has something to do with that place over on the Mogote. It was a school for awhile. You know, that old hotel?"

"What about it—what kind of a school was it? I thought it was illegal for foreigners to be involved financially in schools in Mexico."

"Not if the students are all foreigners. These were German girls. College students studying Marine Biology. There was some kind of tie-in with the Mexican Marine Biology College here in La Paz. All that aqua-culture stuff. I went out with a student from over there a couple of times, but it didn't work out because they kept a tight rein on them. She hated the school but her parents were making her attend."

"Was she from the old East Germany part of the country?"

"Huh? I don't know. She said she was from Berlin but I never thought to ask whether it was East or West. Anyway, it's all over now— the school I mean. That's what I was going to tell you. They sold the property. Rumor is, some outfit from Las Vegas bought it and they're going to open it up as a hotel again as soon as they remodel it. Chuck, the new manager of the *La Posada*, was talking about it after he got drunk the other night. He's drinking up the profits—looks like to me. Anyway, strange that two hotels in La Paz are being taken over by people from Las Vegas. I mean that school was once a hotel. How the hell do they expect to make any money over on the Mogote? It's weird. But what do I know about the hotel business? I can't even afford to spend a night in one. Not that I'd want to. I don't know why anyone would want to pay a lot of money just to sleep in a room. It's like paying for a woman. Oh, well. Guess there are lots of hookers in Vegas, too. Beats me."

Our food came and I let the matter drop. He seemed glad to change the subject. I guess he hoped his rambling would get my mind off Antiay. It wasn't working, but I appreciated the effort.

We ate and talked about La Paz, his art, and the diving out at *Espíritu Santo* Island. I finally excused myself and paid the bill. He said he was waiting around to meet some lady who was staying down at the *Los Arcos* Hotel. She'd seen his work in the gift shop and wanted to meet the artist. His friend in the store told him she was very beautiful, if a little plump, so of course Hal had left her a message to meet him at the *La Terraza*. Good old Hal—he'd bend over backwards for his patrons. At least if they were female.

I got on the Hog and rode home. I'd already thanked Pepe and Lourdes for their hospitality and told them I'd be staying at home tonight. They'd been great, but all of this talk about murder and drugs had to be upsetting for them. I didn't want to disrupt their lives any more than necessary.

I wasn't much company for anyone right now. I really preferred to be alone with my thoughts about Antiay. The bad part was that the good memories I had of her, kept getting edged out by the looped replay of the body on the bed. Then for a minute or two my mind would start running through all the if-onlys...if only I'd got there sooner...if only I hadn't let her leave... Then I'd realize what I was doing and make myself think of something else. I could put on a good tough guy front around friends, but I was really starting to get a bit wacko.

As I walked in the door of my house, I had second thoughts about being alone. This business was giving me the creeps and it had been nice to be around some normal, happy, everyday family people for a change. Then I stumbled over something where nothing should be.

"What the—"

"Hold it right there," a voice said, accompanied by what sounded like the hammer click of a revolver.

I froze as a light came on and I found myself staring down the black hole of a .38 Smith & Wesson.

"Mr. Sage. I was hoping it was you."

Chapter Seven

HE HAD ME cold. I could have done a triple roll and come up firing right after I heard the click of the hammer, and before the light came on. Course that would mean I'd have to be packing the cannon, which I wasn't. And his eyes were adjusted to the dark and could see me in the moonlight streaming through the west-facing window, while my eyes hadn't even seen the contents of my drawers and shelves tossed on the floor like the room had drunk too much tequila and puked all over itself.

Of course it was a good thing I wasn't carrying because if I'd poked .45 caliber holes in the governor's Executive Assistant, the best I could look forward to would be hiding out for the rest of my life in some cabin in the Aleutian Islands. That's supposing I got away.

"Did you find anything you liked *Señor Flores?*"

I knew Rafael Flores pretty well. He was the governor's shadow. In fact, he really ran the show. He put away the gun, which was comforting.

"I'm afraid I can't claim the credit for redecorating your home. That's why I aimed the gun at you. Until I turned the light on, I wasn't sure it was you. I thought they might have returned."

"In that case, please pardon the mess. What can I do for you?"

"The governor would like to talk with you. It is urgent and it is important that no one else know about the meeting. Will you go with me now please?"

"Yeah, sure. But what about the two guys in the white Ford who are watching this place? Did they see you come in?"

"No. I took a taxi and got out two streets away. Then I climbed over the wall and came in the back way. May I use your telephone to call the governor?"

"Sure. But it might be tapped."

"That is no problem. We made arrangements."

I found the phone under the mattress which had been thrown off the bed.

"Here you go."

"Thank you." He dialed a number. "One hour," is all he said into the phone before he hung up. "I will give you directions once we are away from here. I will ride with you if that is possible."

"Okay, but we had better disguise you."

I rummaged around and found the motorcycle helmet I almost never wore. Before I handed it to him, I checked inside for scorpions. They love dark, warm places to nest. He put on the helmet and we went outside. I opened the gate and fired up the Hog, then motioned for him to climb on. I took his arms and wrapped them around my stomach so he'd know I meant for him to hang on, and I gunned the Hog into the street heading straight at the Ford. They tried to duck down, but the headlight caught them looking like Laurel and Hardy as we roared past. We were probably several blocks away before they could even try to follow us, but they could radio others to be on the lookout. La Paz is small enough that my Harley stands out like an elephant in Topeka, so I decided to pull a switch.

My good friends, Wally and Tina Burr were out sailing on their boat, the Dawn Treader. They had given me the key to their garage and their old Toyota pick-up just in case I needed a vehicle for something like taking my propane tank to be refilled. It had happened before. They were nice people.

I took back streets and at least six dogs chased *Señor Flores'* ankles, but I outran all of them. It's quite a sight if you're not used to it—those snarling fangs a few inches from your pants-leg. Then we pulled up in front of the garage. Wally and Tina lived in an old Hacienda they'd rebuilt. It was a wonderful place with an old windmill that still worked. But there had been no off-street parking, since the house was on a hill up above the street. So Wally dug a garage back into the hill and built walls made out of that pink stone they have so much of down here. He'd built it big enough so he could have his woodshop at the back end, and when you walked in, the smell of sawdust was in the air.

I parked the Hog, slid open the garage door and drove the Toyota into the street. Then I put the Hog inside and locked the door again. No one had driven down the street, so I figured we'd made the switch without being detected. *Señor Flores* hadn't said a word throughout the whole process. He was used to working quietly in the background until needed.

When we got in the pick-up I asked him where we were going.

"Do you know the road to *Los Planes?*" he asked.

"Yeah sure." I started up the old Toyota and started to drive. "What does the governor want anyway?"

"I'm sure he would wish to tell you himself."

Meeting the governor out in the desert in the middle of the night was a sure indication I was getting somewhere. It was 1:20 a.m. now and we still had 45 minutes until we were to meet. I checked the gas gauge. Good old Wally. The tank was nearly full.

The road to *Los Planes* only went about forty miles and ended at a bay called *Los Muertos*, which means the Bay of the Dead. I hoped we weren't going that far. That was the thing about this case. It jerked me along all over the place and every time I turned around another strange angle popped up, like shadows on a dark street. Starting tomorrow I was going to do some of my own jerking around. I didn't know yet if I'd tell the governor that I was going to see his son. Blood was thicker than good sense sometimes and I thought maybe it was better if the gov didn't know. I'd play it by ear. The last time I had spoken with the governor, the night Antiay was murdered, I got the very clear impression that I was to be a non-person in the governor's future-book. Yeah well, time heals all wounds, even mortal ones. I'd forgive him for that little faux pas.

The road to *Los Planes* is a straight run out of La Paz, so I could easily tell if anyone had picked up our trail. It goes up a grade for twenty miles until it crosses a pass over the small mountains that create a semicircle around the city. We were nearing the top of the climb, and in the light of the full moon you could see all of La Paz, the bay, and the Sea of Cortez clear past *Espíritu Santo* Island. It was a beautiful sight even in a rear view mirror. I had ridden the Hog out here many times, more than a few with Antiay. Oh babe...

"Turn left up ahead," said Flores.

"The dam?" I asked.

"Yes, the dam, please."

I turned onto the dirt road that wound up through the cactus. Now this was a place for a clandestine meeting that would be great in a movie. We bounced the half-mile up the rugged dirt road until it ended overlooking a river gorge. I stopped the car and we got out, taking in the moonlit view. It was a good thing I wasn't the nervous type. There was a good chance they wanted to get rid of me, and the next time I saw the gov, we would be toasted marshmallows singing camp songs for the devil.

"Hot damn!" I said. "This would be a great place for a shootout in a movie, don't you think so, Rafael?"

"You have too much imagination *Señor* Sage. Please follow me," and he marched off down the trail. Yeah. He was right. I had just too much imagination for my own good. Why couldn't I be happy with real bullets and bloody corpses? There seemed to be enough of those around. Did I have to make them up, too?

I followed him along the trail to the steps leading down onto the top of the concrete dam, and tried to make conversation.

"The dam sure is beautiful in the moonlight."

He didn't answer and continued down the steps. When we reached the top of the dam he finally spoke.

"We will wait here. The governor will arrive soon."

He obviously didn't want to talk so I decided to enjoy the scenery. The *Buena Mujer* dam is about two hundred feet high and a thousand feet across. It's not the kind of dam that is meant to be a reservoir. There is no huge lake backed up behind it. That's the surprising thing. You look down and there's just a creek running through a mix of palm trees and cactus. The dam is intended to hold back the run-off during the rainy season, July through December, when hurricanes or their remnants follow their historic path across the tip of Baja. The dam keeps all of that precious water from just rushing down to the Sea of Cortez, and forces it to seep into the natural underground lakes beneath the mountains where it becomes the fresh water supply for La Paz. It's a beautiful system.

I'd heard there are several dams but this is the only one I'd seen. They used to be earthen, but this concrete dam was built after the disaster of 1976. That year, an exceptionally strong hurricane hit the area. One of the earthen dams became weakened by the amount of water building up behind it. For some reason the government officials decided it would be better to blow up a portion of the dam in order to control the flow. Someone once told me they did it to divert the water away from downtown La Paz, where the expensive property is, and into the impoverished areas. I don't know. But the resulting flood did engulf a poorer barrio, and up to ten thousand people were drowned.

As I looked out across the magnificent arroyo glowing in the moonlight, I understood that, for most people, the murder of one *gringa* woman paled in significance to the deaths of ten thousand innocent people. But not for me. I knew her murder was just one of thousands of victims worldwide who died of violence the same night she did. In this century, more Americans were murdered with handguns in the United States than there were American servicemen killed in all foreign wars combined. In a perverse way, I felt that every murderer I caught was equally responsible for murders committed worldwide. Call it biblical justice, call it anything you want. For me, it meant no mercy for killers.

I'd always taken murder personally—ever since that morning when I was four years old, and I'd awakened and gone downstairs to find my mom and dad lying in bed with their throats cut. When I grew up and solved my first murder, it felt like some kind of answer. Even after fifteen years, when I got tired of it all and needed a rest, I knew I'd go on eventually. Solving murder was a part of me and I was good at it. It was a struggle I'd been born to, my own private yin and yang. When I'd tried to escape it, it followed me here to La Paz and made it personal once again. Now I had to solve Antiay's murder, even if in solving it I destroyed the love I'd known.

I looked up from the arroyo and stared into the shadows of the mountainside. Antiay...Antiay. The desolate beauty of the mountains was just a mirage covering the black hole of emptiness it really was, like an echo of her laughter. For a moment I thought I heard that echo, but it changed into the clatter and whoosh of a helicopter.

Startled, I jumped back from the railing over which I'd been leaning. I darted a glance at *Señor Flores* but he was calm. The helicopter was evidently what he had been waiting for. "It's the governor," he said. "Let's go."

The helicopter appeared to land on the hill above the other side of the dam. You couldn't walk all the way across the dam because the walkway stopped near the center where the spillway allowed water to flow over the dam before it reached the top. I knew there was a tunnel with stairs inside the dam that descended to the bottom, went underneath the dam and came up on the other side. I'd been down there with Antiay, until the bats flying over our heads creeped us out too much, and we'd hurried back out.

Sure enough, that's where *Señor Flores* led me. He didn't seem to be too excited about the prospect, because as he switched on the flashlight he'd brought and we began to descend the two hundred feet of unlit stairs into the bowels of the dam, he began to alternately curse and pray in Spanish. I couldn't resist whispering a few words about, "*Muy peligroso. Muchos murciélagos aqui,*" which means in bad Spanish—very dangerous, many bats here.

Flores brought us here, so whatever the governor wanted to talk about must be important and dangerous, to have taken such precautions to keep it a secret. Granted I had become, somehow, *persona non gratis* in official circles. But was it really necessary to descend all the way into hell to meet?

I'd soon find out. We reached the bottom of the stairs and walked along the flat stretch for about two hundred feet before he whispered, "Stop. We'll wait here."

It seemed like forever, but it was probably only a couple of minutes before we could make out a dim light approaching from the other direction. The tunnel was like a tomb and it was so dark the shadows almost swallowed the flashlight beam. Finally, I recognized the governor's voice booming out from the dark. It was then I realized Flores and I had been whispering for some silly reason. Just the atmosphere of the place I guess.

"Is that you Rick?" the governor asked.

"It's me all right, and *Señor Flores.*"

I couldn't see his face in the dark, but his voice was full of tension. He aimed the flashlight at me for an instant.

"Sorry, Rick. I wondered how bad it was. They worked you over good."

"You heard?"

"Yes, but not directly. I have my sources though."

"Yeah well, I got my licks in, too."

"I heard that also. You are a stubborn man."

"That's mostly what it takes for my line of work."

"I suppose so. Still, to be always a companion of death must be very difficult."

I felt like saying that it beat politics, but I didn't. "What can I do for you, sir?"

"Do you remember my son?" he didn't wait for me to answer. "He has been killed. Shot. A few hours ago."

I heard the sadness in his voice. Guess I could cancel that Mazatlán trip. Someone was staying one jump ahead of me. "Damn. I'm sorry. Really sorry. I know you were very close."

"Not so close the last couple of years I'm afraid. He had fallen in with bad company again. He was a good boy once, but it seems he was a very weak man. Even so, I loved him very much."

I heard tears in his voice. "I understand your grief, sir, but what does this have to do with me? If you wanted my help, well, I'm afraid I have my hands full already. Besides you have the entire—"

"You will understand in a moment. Like they say, a picture is worth a thousand words. I received this in the mail the same day your girlfriend was murdered."

He handed me a photograph and his flashlight.

"At the time, I didn't realize the connection. My son was in Mazatlan, your—"

His voice seemed distant—like a fading voice-over in a film noir. I studied the picture, but it kept fading on me, too. The air in the tunnel suddenly seemed stifling, like a room without air. I couldn't get my breath. Was this a dream or what?

My legs felt weak. Yeah it was her all right. Her and Victor, the governor's son. They were lying naked, propped up against pillows on a bed. She was grinning and holding a mirror on which were lines of white powder, and Victor held a tooter to his nose ready to snort some. Two other naked people were tooting white powder from a table beside the bed, and there were other grinning, naked people around them. I took in all the details. It looked like a sleazy hotel room, like the one she was murdered in. I even looked for the bracelet I'd given her, but her arm was wrapped around Victor.

Damn you, Antiay. Damn you. Who were you really?

It was the grin that was going to haunt me. The grin of the living dead. No sparkle in the eyes, nor her smile—just that zombie-like grin.

"I don't understand," I said—even though I did, in some unreal sense.

I heard the governor again, booming out of the shadows, like a voice in a Stephen King nightmare. I wanted to be alone, but the voice droned on.

"I think the photograph was intended as a threat against me. Blackmail. That is all I understand," the governor said.

He took the photograph out of my hand and the flame of a cigarette lighter appeared next to it. The smell of the burning picture was hellish. I felt like I was going to puke.

"We have both lost someone we loved," the governor said, as pure, red-hot anger began to overtake the sick feeling in my stomach.

"But what is worse, they have murdered our memories...you must find—"

"Tell me what you know about this, you bastard," I screamed. As I lunged at the governor, I heard the hammer-click of the .38 for the second time that night. That was one time too many. I whirled, and with one hand on the governor, shined the flashlight in Flores eyes and kicked the side of his head. He crumpled to the floor.

I pushed the governor up against the wall. "Now you fucking bastard—I don't care if you're the Queen of England—you're going to goddamn tell me what the fuck this fucking goddamn mess is all about or I'll leave enough blood here from you and your pal to feed a mountain of vampire bats. I want some goddamn answers and I want them—"

Suddenly the rage was spent, and I felt like that Sisyphus guy at the top of the mountain with nothing left to do but climb down and start all over again. I let the governor off the wall.

"Damn," I said.

"I came here to tell you what I can—"

"Yeah, I know. I just went crazy. I'm sorry about your son. If you'd leveled with me two days ago though, he might still be alive."

"Rick, please believe me. Two days ago I didn't understand."

We slumped against opposite walls of the tunnel and sat on the concrete floor. Flores was already there, propped up and holding his head.

"Tell me," I whispered.

"A few months ago," the governor began, "the President of Mexico and his advisors secretly decided to allow casino-type gambling in Mexico. Certain interested parties, including some from the North, have been pushing for this for years. Those parties were informed of the decision, along with a few other potential investors. The government feels it will be a good source of income but they are afraid it will cause problems. So they want to isolate it—like your Las Vegas. In Baja Sur we need the source of revenue and the jobs. Also, we have been isolated historically from the mainland. Anyway, the President's plan was to allow a trial period of five years, for one license for one casino. After that, if everything worked out and the people accepted it, La Paz would become like Las Vegas."

"Hold it, let me guess. And you are to choose who gets the trial license, right?"

"That's correct. The President didn't want to offend anyone so he called it a local matter and gave me the responsibility of deciding. There has been much pressure. There is a group of...um...investors from Las Vegas who bought a local hotel recently—"

"Over on the Mogote."

"You have heard. They are represented by a *Señor* Grossman, who is of German nationality. He is evidently also an investor. Certain elements of your government and of mine have been lobbying for this investment group."

"The DEA?" I asked, amazed once again.

"Yes, your DEA, and others. They seem to have some connection to this Grossman."

"Who else is interested in the license?"

"Of course all of the hotel groups would like to have it. My preference is that it go to one of our Mexican owners. There was so much pressure that I suggested a multi-national partnership, but no one would agree to be the minor partner. We have seen your *Godfather* movie. Partners in Las Vegas have a short life span."

"Yeah. Smart thinking."

"Then I received the photograph, and later a phone call telling me to give the license to the Mogote Group."

"Did the person who called speak in English?"

"Yes."

"With an accent?"

"It was a man, but the voice was disguised so I couldn't be sure."

"What did he say?"

"He said that my family would be very disappointed if the Mogote Group failed to receive the casino license. Then he asked if I liked the photograph of my son, and he hung up."

"What did you do then?"

"I tried again for a compromise among the investor groups. And I called the President and told him I was receiving a lot of pressure to choose the North American Group. He said he understood and it was up to me. He also said that perhaps the North Americans had more experience and resources for such an enterprise."

"So the President is in favor of the Mogote Group, too?"

"It seems so. But I am resisting. This license would be very good for friends of mine. Besides, I don't like the Mogote Group. I don't like this Grossman and his connection with your government. Also, I don't want our state to be run by the godfathers, like your Nevada. There are bad people in our state, too, but at least they are our bad people."

"So you are going to choose a local group?"

"I was. Before my son was murdered. At nine o'clock tonight the governor of Sinaloa called to say they had just found my son dead and there were drugs involved, but they would try to keep it quiet. Then, an hour later I received another call from the same individual who had called about the photograph. He said it was too bad about my son, but I had three days to announce the Mogote Group or the other members of my family would be as disappointed as my son, and then he hung up again.

"Before, I thought they were bluffing, but now I know they are not. So I decided to talk with you. Rick, if you can find out who the murderer is before three days are up, perhaps we can stop the Mogote Group. Otherwise I must choose them. In five years, they will probably be here anyway. But who knows what will happen by then?"

"Governor, I don't really give a damn who gets the casino license. It will ruin Baja Sur anyway, but that's your problem. You believe the same person murdered Antiay and Victor. Maybe. Maybe not. Whoever it was, they are involved in this gambling mess, that seems to be a fact. I'm going to get to the bottom of this, and I don't care who gets hurt doing it. I wish I could say I had a handle on it. But I don't. All I really know is that I didn't know the woman in that picture or the one who ended up a corpse in that cheap hotel. It wasn't the Antiay I knew. Not even close."

"To use your words, Rick, that is your problem. My problem is keeping my family alive. I don't trust anyone around me except Flores here. They might have bought off anyone. They certainly seem to know a lot about me, and they knew I wasn't going to choose them or they wouldn't have murdered my son. That's why I wanted to meet you here. So please don't try to contact me. If you need to talk, contact Flores and use the code word Mogote."

I stood up and started to walk down the tunnel toward the stairs to the pick-up. I kept the governor's flashlight.

"*Hasta luego*," I said, maybe to the bats.

"*Hasta luego*," came back the echo. "*Buena suerte, mi amigo.*"

Good luck, he says. Yeah, I was having loads of that, wasn't I?

Chapter Eight

I REACHED THE pick-up, got in, and drove toward the highway. It wasn't until my head tried to dent the roof that I realized I was going too fast. It wasn't even my vehicle. What the hell was I trying to do? There were easier ways to kill myself.

I turned onto the highway, but after I ground the gears a second time, I looked for a place to pull over. My mind was churning and I just couldn't drive. It was still a beautiful night, with the full moon shining over La Paz Bay in the distance. I rested my arms on the steering wheel and leaned forward, staring into the distant landscape. I felt betrayed, confused and very much alone. Like the flaming photo had cauterized the wound, sealing in the despair. On the outside it all seemed to make some kind of weird sense, but inside it didn't. Inside it was as illogical as war. I couldn't even cry now.

The governor had been right about one thing. First they had murdered Antiay. And now they were killing off my memories of her. It wasn't just that she had a secret past. That photograph could have been a couple of years old. And we never felt a need to rehash other lovers, past or present. Sure it bothered me to see that picture being handed around like old copies of *Hustler*. Whoever had called the governor was like an obscene phone caller talking to your child, and I wanted to reach into that phone and grab the caller's balls and squeeze them in a rusty vise. It was an extremely satisfying idea. I'd try to remember it when I finally caught the bastard.

My mind chased itself around a very short track. It wasn't that Antiay had been stop-actioned in the middle of an orgy that really made me sick either. I didn't like it, but I believe that what people do with their own bodies is their own business. And she had changed. She had quit the drugs and left the bastard.

What was killing me, inside, was the enormity of the lie. All these undeniable revelations of her secret life were destroying the Antiay I knew. The new person I was discovering just couldn't coexist with the old one. One had to be a lie.

I left the lights on, got out, and walked down the road. The fresh air felt good. The Antiay I had thought I knew, taught English at a small private school and all of her students loved her, from the kids in her afternoon classes to the adults in the evening. She was a gentle person, always trying to help someone. Although she didn't make much money herself, she had secretly given money to help with the medical bills of a little girl who had needed extensive corrective surgery to enable her to speak. And she had taken up a collection. I know because I was the first donor.

The sweet smell of the desert night blooming in the shadows reminded me of Antiay. She was a very private person in her social life. Not the type of person to be involved with criminal types. Oh, she liked rebels, misfits and eccentrics—she liked me didn't she? But violent criminal types? Never. She didn't believe in violence and was always trying to smooth off some of my rough edges.

I hadn't known much about her past, but I did know she had been hurt once. Something had happened that made her stare off sometimes and start to cry. When I asked her what was bothering her, she only said, "I can't talk about it yet—maybe someday."

Was what I'd learned tonight the secret she'd never been able to tell me? Or was there more? I didn't know. I didn't even know if my Antiay was real. If I'd been some other detective on this case, someone who didn't know my Antiay, her death would probably look like the usual falling out over drug money. Maybe that was my problem. I was just too close to it all. I couldn't be objective. Instead of cooperating with the police who were investigating the case, I'd managed to get in a brawl with them. Sure they were dickheads, but I've worked with dickheads before— lots of them. I hadn't even really examined the scene of the crime, or the body for that matter.

A car crested the hill behind the pick-up, and I slipped in amongst the Cardón cactus alongside the road. I didn't want to explain to some helpful soul what I was doing here. I didn't want to talk to anyone— maybe ever. The car passed and I tried to re-board my train of thought.

The body. Christ! It had been four days and I hadn't even thought about that. Jesus! The body! What about funeral arrangements? What would they have done? A pauper's grave? I didn't know anything about her family—it seemed part of what she hadn't wanted to talk about. What would they have done about the body? The German Consulate in Mexico City? Maybe. Damn though, I should have taken care of it.

Maybe I was in some kind of shock. I'd seen it before in others...doing crazy things...like this one woman whose husband had died of a heart attack. She took some dirty clothes in a laundry bag and started driving on a cross-country trip. She was reported missing, and when I finally caught up with her she said she didn't know why she'd done it, just that she and her husband had been planning to make that trip someday.

I started back toward the pick-up and kicked a beer can into the road. Okay. I was going to snap out of it and start acting like a detective again. I wasn't going to wait around anymore for things to come to me. After I called the Old Prof about Grossman tomorrow, I'd revisit the scene of the crime. Then I'd check on the body. After that, White. And then this guy Grossman, who seemed to be looming larger and larger in this case.

I reached the pick-up just as the first light of dawn cracked the horizon. It had been a long night. I put the key in the ignition and turned it. The starter turned once, slowly, and began to click. Dead battery. Yeah well, it was twenty miles to La Paz, all downhill. It would surely jumpstart before that. I got out of the pick-up and started to push myself toward the new day.

I'D ARRIVED HOME at 5:30 a.m. It was five minutes after ten now, and I was still groggy with sleep. I didn't think I'd dreamed, and I was grateful for that. I probably hadn't slept long enough to get into the heavy stuff.

I slipped into my sandals and shuffled through the mess to make coffee. I'd got in the habit of not putting on my shoes first thing, although they were worn and comfortable enough to wear like sandals. The thing is, it's a good idea to knock your shoes together a couple of times down here, just to make sure scorpions haven't checked in for the night. The scorpions are mostly little guys—they won't kill you unless you're allergic to them. Their sting is kind of like a bee sting, but it's a rude awakening nonetheless.

Luckily whoever had searched my place hadn't messed much with the kitchen. The coffee maker was still in one piece. I filled it with water, dumped about the right amount of grounds into the filter, and stuck my cup under the magical hole where the coffee came out. That way the first cup is almost strong enough to be called espresso. The only trouble with this method is, you have to concentrate on what you're doing and I'm not very good at that first thing in the morning. I couldn't count the times I'd wandered off and let the cup overflow all over the counter. This morning I kept my two fingers on the handle and when it was full, I switched the cup with the coffeepot. *Voilà!* The morning was starting off okay.

I checked the hole under the loose tile where I kept the cannon and ammo hid, and they were still there. I wasn't surprised because I'd done a good job of camouflage. The cannon and holsters were wrapped in an oil soaked towel and were just as I'd left them. The hole was sealed pretty tight so I didn't think insects could get in there, but just to make sure I didn't accidentally meet up with a scorpion or a black widow spider when

I reached my hand in, I kept a couple of Shell No-Pest Strips in there, too.

I put the cannon back in the hole, replaced the tile and put the nightstand on top of it. I didn't think I needed to carry the gun—not yet anyway. I didn't get a Mexican permit for it when I came down here, although I could have gotten one easily enough with the governor's help. I hadn't believed I would need a weapon, let alone a permit. But the cannon was a part of me, a tool of the trade, like a writer's pen. The cannon existed in and of itself, the permit was only for using it, legally. Like a marriage license. Yeah, that's exactly how I felt about it—all of that bureaucratic bullshit. Like the P.I. license which had different requirements in every State. I wasn't a detective because there was some government position to be filled and I had applied for the job. I chased down murderers because I believed anyone who would do mortal violence to another human being should be eliminated, or at least incarcerated for the rest of their lives. And, I did it because I was good at it. The permits, the licenses, the permission from mother—a spanking was the least of my troubles right now.

I sat down on the bed, picked up the telephone, and dialed the Old Prof. I didn't know how long it would take me to get through to him. Like I said, he had a thing about telephones. In his office at the University he kept the telephone in a drawer of his desk so he would barely hear it ringing. That way he could ignore it if he was having a conversation with someone. I knew how he felt. Before the advent of answering machines, people had got in the habit of letting a telephone call interrupt whatever they were doing. Nine point three seconds to simultaneous orgasm, and the phone would ring. Both parties would say, "I'll get it," and reach for the damn thing.

This morning, for the first time since I'd known him, Fred actually picked up the phone on the second ring. "Fred, is that you?"

"It sure is Rick. I was hoping this was you. How are you?"

Fred is a calm guy. But this morning I sensed tension in his voice, although that would never stop him from carrying on in his calm, polite manner. "Well Fred," I said, "I've got a tiger by the balls, but as long as I don't lose my grip on things, I'll be all right. How about yourself?"

"Oh, I'm fine—same as always. Say, I did some checking as you asked, and I hit the jackpot. You really do have a tiger in hand this time."

"Whatcha got?"

"I called an old friend who is still active. He wasn't in so I left a message—'Dr. Metcalf calling about Jurgen Grossman'. An hour and a half later he called me back and told me to go to a phone booth, and he gave me the number of another booth where he'd be waiting for my call.

Of course he didn't say it in those words. We used to work together and I
knew what he meant. Even the phone number I was to call was in our old
code. It was kind of fun, I have to admit. Like old times."

"Are you thinking of going back in?"

"No, no. It wasn't that much fun. Anyway, I went to a phone booth
on a corner by a gas station and called him. He wanted to know what in
the hell I was involved in. Those are almost his exact words. He said
Grossman was a bad character and wanted to know what this was all
about. I told him it was about murder, Grossman might be involved, and I
was calling for a friend who was in Mexico. He said okay, he'd tell me
what he knew, but off the record of course. That was an old joke between
us. As far as the CIA goes, there is no on the record. There is no record,
period."

"Sounds like this guy, Grossman, has really been around."

"You're not kidding. Wait until you hear the rest of the story. My
friend verified that Grossman had once worked for East German
Intelligence. Stasi. I won't go into all the details because this phone call is
going to cost a fortune as it is. But basically, Grossman and his pals beat
old Gorbachev to capitalism by a few years. When the wall finally fell,
they already had a big market share in the arms business."

"And they sold to both sides?"

"You've got it. Anyone with cash. They sold to Nicaragua and they
sold to the Contras, who used CIA money funneled to them secretly
during the years when Congress shut off official support of the Contras."

"Like during the Iran-Contra scandal time-period?"

"Yes, exactly. In fact, that's the big secret the Iran-Contra hearings
never unearthed. They were close when they found out about the Costa
Rican drug connection. Remember?"

"Yeah, the secret airfield on the big *gringo*-owned ranch in Costa
Rica."

"Yes, that's it. But the Company did a good job of burying that one.
Grossman was involved in all of that business. He had the drug
connections because the emerging cocaine cartels were buying arms from
him and using them to trade for protection with communist guerillas in
Columbia, Peru, and so forth."

"And they basically did the same thing with the Contras?"

"More or less. With the Contras through the CIA. The Contras really
didn't have much to offer. But the CIA did. Noriega, in Panama, for
instance. The CIA was the facilitator. Like in Southeast Asia with the
heroin traffickers during the Vietnam era. This kind of thing is why I got
out of the Company. When I started, the saying was, does the end justify

the means? It was a question, which was bad enough. After awhile it became no longer a question, just ... the end justifies the means."

"Yeah, I've heard murderers say more or less the same thing."

"Exactly. To get back to Grossman, after Perestroika, the CIA decided they didn't need Grossman anymore. In fact, the connection had become something of an embarrassment. The Cold War had turned into the War on Drugs. Noriega and the cocaine cartels had become a major liability."

"It took them long enough to figure that out."

"You have to understand that we had a history of dealing with such people. The Company had used criminal groups since its conception. In France, and with the Mafia since the beginning of World War Two in Sicily. Anyway, the CIA turned the Grossman connection over to the DEA."

"To prosecute?"

"Oh, no. So the DEA could use his connections. They made some kind of deal with him. I suppose some kind of concessions in exchange for information on the cartels. My friend at the Company didn't know any details. They've washed their hands of him, more or less."

"Yeah, more or less—until the next time. You must be close friends with this guy for him to give you so much info."

"We're like brothers. I saved his life once. Oh, nothing too heroic, but we've been close ever since. And he said he met this Grossman once, and didn't like him. Scum of the earth, is actually what he said. If you can convict him of murder, so much the better, but he said to tell you to watch out. This guy is ruthless and has a lot of connections. And, the information I've just relayed doesn't exist. Understand?"

"Yeah, sure. Everything in this case has been deniable. When I catch the guy who murdered Antiay, I'm going to deny I enjoyed crushing his nuts in a rusty vise, too."

"I'm sorry Rick, but that's the best I could do."

"Hey, this information is a big help. I didn't expect half as much. It's just that I was very close to...the victim. I'm a little emotional about it."

"I'm glad I could help. Maybe when it's over we can go sailing. It might be good medicine—always seems to do wonders for me."

"Yeah sure. It might at that. Thanks again."

We said goodbye and hung up. I didn't know if Grossman was responsible for Antiay's death. But he had definitely become a player in the game. And the information Fred gave me cleared up the DEA connection at least. Fred may not have been a James Bond type, but it seems he had been more of a spook than he'd ever let on before. And his friend had really stuck his neck out. I hoped I wouldn't let him down. If I did it wouldn't be because I hadn't died trying.

I showered, chugged another cup of coffee, shaved, brushed my teeth, and combed my hair, all in a trance. In my mind's eye all I could see was a gradually materializing image—like the reflection in a mirror as the fog on the glass starts to evaporate minutes after a hot shower. I wanted to reach into the fog, grasp the unformed neck in my hands and squeeze until I felt a dead weight along the taut muscles of my outstretched arms. I smiled, and if someone had seen that smile they probably would have thought me more than a little crazy. After all, I hadn't even met him yet and already I hated him. Jurgen Grossman—a gross man.

I dressed and topped it off with a fresh cotton bowling shirt. They were perfect for the heat down here. Even better than in L.A. I owned about thirty of them, all with different first names above the shirt pocket, and fictional bowling alley logos across the back. They were great uniforms for a detective. People looked at the name and if it said 'Bob', why you must be Bob all right. This one said Hank and it was purple. It was the color I imagined Grossman's face would turn when I choked him.

I hoped to finally meet him today—he was on my list. But that would be later. First on the list was another face I'd like to do a chameleon number on—Bill White.

I checked everything with a glance, shut off the coffee, and walked out the door, leaving the mess for Guille, the maid. I hoped she wouldn't quit on me. More likely she would just smile. She worked by the hour. And she was worth every minute.

I stopped outside for a moment to admire the bougainvillea. They went well with my shirt. Too bad. I was in the mood for a clash.

I fired up the Hog and headed for the *Gran Baja* Hotel. It was only a few blocks away, just up the beach north of the *La Posada* Hotel. I could see the top half of its eleven floors as I rode along the street.

It's the largest hotel in La Paz and has the best view from its rooms. It also has the largest swimming pool. I swim there often. They have a policy—if you buy a few drinks you can swim in their pool, as long as you don't bother the registered guests. It's a nice arrangement.

The *Gran Baja* had been given a new coat of paint less than a year ago. The new paint is one of those colors in the old big Crayola box, somewhere between something like burnt umber and salmon pink. When we were kids we used to call that color 'titty pink', but being older and wiser now, I know that all depends on whose you're talking about. Anyway, it seems like a good color for a resort hotel. Probably even why they picked it. Before that it had never had a paint job. It had looked, from a distance, like the world's largest parking garage. Except for all the windows of course.

The thing about the *Gran Baja's* new paint job, is that during that same time period, Antiay and I were caught up in the heat of rising passion. That tropical storm feel of thunder, lightning, warm rain and high humidity that causes desert blossoms to burst out uncontrollably, in wanton satisfaction of a long unfulfilled need...an almost insufferable itch to be relieved.

That first passion of blooming love fertilized with lust, almost cannot be described. It must be experienced—consumed—and we often found ourselves in unusual situations, where moments earlier we had been discussing, say, a type of wine for our dinner. Then some touch, like a passing brush of leg against leg, would set us scrambling for a secret place nearby where we could shed our street identities. Like Superman and Wonder Woman meeting in the same closet we'd struggle with each other's buttons, belts, catches and tongues in barely concealed nooks and crannies.

It was in one of those storms that we found ourselves opening a janitor's closet on the top floor of the *Gran Baja*. To our surprise the closet ceiling had an unlocked hatch overhead. Since we had practically fallen into the closet in lust, it took us a moment to untangle tongues and mumble, "up there." I boosted her, with feeling, and pulled myself up to a panoramic view that ignited the explosive passions we'd carried with us. We did it there on the roof, and when the sunset came later, it was like the world offering us a rose.

That's why I felt so much disgust as I parked the Hog in the *Gran Baja's* parking lot. Bill White staying in this place was like worms chewing at Antiay's coffin, and I had to struggle to choke back my emotions.

"You're a private investigator and you're trying to solve a case of murder," I said aloud to myself as I made my way up the stairs to the lobby. "You are not a lover seeking revenge, you're the iceman."

Except the ice kept melting.

I already knew which room White would be in so I didn't stop at the desk. I pushed the elevator call button, the doors opened, I stepped in and pushed the number 11. He'd be on the top floor, in the double suite on the corner. The one with a view over-looking La Paz and the Bay. The DEA always took the best room with a view. To be fair, it fit their undercover role of high rolers. Confiscated money from drug busts paid for the luxury. That was fine, except the agents became used to that style of living and came to expect it after awhile. Like the undercover people who used

cocaine for show. After awhile they started to like it. It was a very
corrupting method of investigation.

I took a deep breath, for control, and knocked on the door. After the
time it takes someone to walk across a room, the door opened. It was an
agent I hadn't met, but obviously DEA. "What can I do for you Mr. ..?"

"Sage. Rick Sage. I want to talk to your boss, Bill White."

"Sage, huh? I'm afraid Mr. White is very busy and doesn't have
time—"

He started to close the door but was stopped by my number thirteen
clodhopper. "I said I want to talk to White, Mr. Robatoid," and raised the
ante with a shoulder thrust to the door. It flew open and the agent sprawled
across one of the extra single beds they'd added to the suite. Apparently
White traveled in force. As he lost his balance he tried to cover with
bureaucratic mumbo-jumbo. "We're a Federal Law Enforcement Agency
and you're—"

"This is Mexico, pal, and I'm here on official business." I guessed
that was true in a sense. Last night, the governor had asked for my help,
although he'd most certainly deny it.

He was struggling to upright himself as he tried to get a lock on the
handgun belt-holstered behind his back. I prepared for the kick to send it
flying, and the situation appeared to be deteriorating from hostile
confrontation into outright war. Then diplomacy intervened. In the
doorway between the suites, Bill White appeared, staring coldly at his
agent sprawled on the bed.

"That's all right O'Brien," he said in his best command voice.
"Come in Sage."

I walked toward the other room as the agent gave me a surly look
like some schoolboy who'd been caught with his pants down. I noticed a
bank of radios on a desk, along with a headset and a notepad, and the
naughty schoolboy sat back down to his work as I entered White's inner
sanctum.

The room was large. There was a double bed, several easy chairs, a
wet bar, and a huge desk covered with papers. On one corner of the desk
sat a computer. An expensive pair of binoculars sat on a table near the
balcony, matching the pair on a tripod in the other room.

White stood with his back to me staring out the window. "What do
you want?"

"You know why I'm here."

White turned to face me across his desk. His facial features looked
like they had been chiseled out of stone, and ordinarily his demeanor was
ambassadorial. Today he seemed on edge. "If it's about that..." He paused

and I could see him weighing me, and then his words. Evidently he had an accurate scale, because I had the distinct impression he had been about to say something derogatory, and I was poised to spring. He changed his mind. "That friend of yours who killed herself over...maybe you should just let sleeping dogs lie."

"You're a lying dog, White. She was murdered and I intend to find out why."

"I understand there may have been drugs involved in her death," he said, the smooth façade falling further. "The rumor is she was a cocaine addict. If you were so close to her you must have known that fact."

"As far as I knew she didn't use drugs, but I didn't come here to discuss her habits. She was murdered. I'll find out who did it, whatever the motive. And it's no longer just one murder victim. Now it's two, and you can throw in blackmail for good measure. How much is your dirty little deal with Grossman worth anyway?"

That caught him short and he turned away, his back to me once again. What an arrogant man. He stared out the full-length windows, trying to regain his composure. "I don't know what you're talking about," he mumbled.

"Let me refresh your memory. Stop me if you care to add anything. Jurgen Grossman, owner of the *Southern Cross*—that big yacht riding at anchor out there in the harbor. Grossman, the international arms dealer, who has connections to the Mafia and the Cocaine Cartels. Jurgen Grossman, whom you've been helping to obtain a gambling license for his hotel over on the Mogote, in exchange for information from him on the cocaine cartels. You've sold your fucking soul to the devil, White, and the sad thing is, it's probably not the first time. People are being murdered, and you just turn your back."

White spun around and pounded the desk with his fist. "If it takes the deaths of a couple of scum drug addicts to put the cartels out of business then I consider that a damn cheap price. Your girlfriend was a slut— they're both sluts."

I leaped forward, but he was ready. He'd already pulled a .38 revolver out of a hiding place beneath the desktop. "Hold it right there, Sage," he said, backing toward the windows.

I stopped, feigning frustration. It wasn't too difficult, because even though the detective side of me wanted to hear what he had to say, a stronger part wanted to leap the desk and kick the self-righteous bastard right through the windows. "So you're the judge and jury now—or do you see yourself as God?"

"I don't have to answer to a two-bit citizen like you, Sage. I'm not going to admit anything to you, but I'll tell you what. This is a war. Do you think we call it the drug war for nothing? Grossman's already given us enough information to badly damage the Colombians. And I'd trade a lot more than a gambling casino to get the cartels. We can control gambling. Maybe we can even get control of Baja. Mexico's just a corrupt third world country. They need our help. We can work with the Mafia. We've done it before. Look at Las Vegas. On the other hand, the cartels hate America. Hell, I'd drop a nuclear bomb on those jungles in Columbia, if the President would let me—you bet your goddamn life. Sure I'd use Grossman, and the devil himself, too."

"It's been tried before, White."

"Be careful, Sage, because even innocent people get killed in war. And that's too bad. It's just too damn bad. Now this interview is terminated, so get out."

He waved his gun at me and I moved toward the door. O'Brien was standing there with a .38 in his hand, too. I had the feeling they'd both be happy to use them so I made my way carefully past O'Brien. "You're sick, White," I said as I let myself out the door. "You're a very, very sick man."

The door closed behind me and I heard O'Brien flick the deadbolt. Paranoid, these guys. As I walked toward the elevator I took my pocket recorder out of its place on my belt. It was still running. Great. I couldn't wait to make copies for all of my friends in high places.

People like White, who thought they had all the answers—the fanatics of all the causes who refused to listen to another person's point of view—were responsible for most of the world's problems.

Meet the Salman Rushdie of Baja. Publish or perish is my motto. Nobody is going to stop me from finding the truth—unless they take a giant step over my dead body.

I collected the Hog from the parking lot and rode down the *Malecón* to the Hotel *Perla*. Freddy's office was there, up the stairs overlooking the Harbor. I wanted to ask him to come with me to the police morgue. His office was closed though—probably still catching up on his homework. I envied him.

I was feeling the first pangs of hunger mixed with a queasy jitteriness that comes from drinking too much coffee and eating no breakfast. Throw in a double shot of adrenaline and you've got a nice prescription for ulcers. I wished I'd gone down the beach from the *Gran Baja* to the *La Posada* for *chilaquiles*, but in the excitement I hadn't been thinking about food. Now my stomach was reminding me.

I decided to eat at the *La Terraza*. It was right next door and their food was passable. Besides, Freddy might come by. If not, I could mellow out a bit watching the boats in the harbor and the *señoritas* passing by on the street....

I slipped into a booth and Hector appeared out of nowhere. "*Señor Sage*, you are feeling better?"

"Huh? Oh yeah, sure Hector." I touched the stitches over my eye. The cut seemed to be healing fine, so I hadn't reapplied the bandages. Too conspicuous. "I'm feeling much better. Guess I better figure out some new moves with my cape-work. The bulls are getting smarter and faster every year."

"Yes, everything seems to move much faster as the years pass and—"

Just then, a beautiful *señorita* flowed past the table, like a plumeria blossom floating down a slow-moving river. A river with many curves and—

Hector interrupted my thoughts. "Like that, you see? We are dreaming and she is already gone." He winked at me. "Better, the bull. What can I get you *mi amigo?*"

I laughed. "I'd like to think she just hasn't caught up to me yet." He laughed back. "I'll have *huevos rancheros con tortillas de harina y dos vasos grande de jugo de naranja, por favor.*"

"*Bueno*," he said and left for the kitchen. I had my restaurant Spanish down pretty good. Unless the waiter tried to test me with a rapid-fire retort. But Hector spoke excellent English. Besides, we were friends of the sort you make when you're a regular customer in a small town. And, I'd helped him out with a drunk *gringo* tourist one night who kept making loud crude suggestions to some *señoritas* seated at a table in the restaurant near the bar.

Hector could have summoned the police, but since the guy was drunk, he tried to give him a break. I had watched from my booth in the restaurant as Hector went over and politely asked the turkey to leave. But the drunk's good sense, if he had any, was too well pickled, and the jerk stood up, cursing loudly.

I slipped over to Hector's side, grabbed the jerk by the arm, whispered some sweet-nothings in his ear as I tightened down my grip, then I showed him the door. I should have thanked the jerk, because he made me quite a few friends. I returned to a standing ovation, a bottle of excellent champagne, and a kiss from each of the *señoritas* who had been hassled.

I had been waiting for Antiay to finish her last class, and by the time she showed up, we had a major party going, with me as the honored guest. When she arrived, they treated her like a visiting queen. She was amazed.

"How do you do it?" she'd asked. "Your Spanish is terrible."

"I don't know," I told her with a smile as we received another toast. "They just sort of took a liking to me. Maybe they think I'm a famous actor or something." Her elbow poked my ribs as we raised our glasses again.

Yeah, like they say, those were the days. A waiter brought orange juice and I downed one of the two glasses. I was thirsty. I put down the glass and my gaze landed on Grossman's yacht, the *Southern Cross*. I wondered if White would warn him I was coming. Probably. I was sure they were in radio contact.

I thought about what White had said. He tried to act confident, but there was something in his manner that seemed more like bluff. I had the feeling he had lost control, and White was a control freak. He didn't like the unexpected. As much as I disliked him, I didn't believe he was involved in the murders. He didn't operate that way, at least directly. But he had known about Victor. Sure, some version of the death of the governor's son was probably in today's papers, but he wasn't surprised at the connection with Antiay. He'd taken it for granted.

A waiter brought the *huevos rancheros* and I began to eat. White had said something strange. What was it? I'd been too busy wanting to break his face to ask him what he'd meant. Part of it had been obvious—he was referring to Antiay. But he'd said, "They're both sluts." Was he saying Victor was a slut, too? Strange choice of words.

They're both sluts. Present tense. I didn't know what it meant, if anything. I could kick myself for not having been under control enough to question him about it. On the other hand, I couldn't really believe I hadn't kicked him through the windows.

I finished eating and downed the other glass of ice cold orange juice. Some freshly squeezed bits of orange gathered on my upper lip and I licked them off.

As I did, I felt someone watching me, and shifted my gaze toward the source. A beautiful brown-eyed woman had been staring at me.

I smiled. She smiled back and looked away. A moment later she looked back and our eyes locked. We smiled again and my engine spun into rpm's way above red-line. I could see those high heels hooked over the rear pegs of the Hog, and the spread of her legs pushing that expensive skirt high up her rich-looking thighs as we roared off.

Hector's bulk suddenly came between us. "Your check, Rick. She is the wife of our mayor. I can introduce you if you like."

Suddenly the Hog was skidding out of control and I dropped the image before it crashed. "There goes your tip, Hector," I said as I grudgingly accepted the bill. When I'd paid it—extra large tip included—he thanked me and moved out of my line of sight.

But the moment had passed. She was engaged in laughing repartee with the other women at the table. It was just as well. Fast Freddy, I wasn't. Oh, if I hadn't known she was married, and to whom... Hey I'm only human.

I walked out of the *La Terraza* and straddled the Hog. I could feel her gaze on me as the Harley engine did its deep bass warm-up solo. When I pulled away from the curb I imagined once again those legs wrapped around me, but it wasn't half a block before Antiay's ghost kicked her rudely out of her seat, bringing back memories of Antiay's body pressed against mine.

It was a short ride to the old hotel where she'd been murdered. I looked for a place to park the Hog. Parking is risky if you own a motorcycle. It's more apt to get banged up in a parking spot than riding down the street. I preferred parking places at the end of a block. That way the only other space was behind the bike and other driver's could see it. This time I found the perfect spot, only halfway into the red zone near the corner. I parked, gave the bike one last look, and walked up the street toward the killing room.

I slipped the manager a few bucks for the key to the room, climbed the stairs and walked to Room 11. What had it been? Three, four days ago? The events stretched out from that scene like blood flowing from a wound. The key worked and I opened the door, half-expecting to see the body still on the bed. I took a deep breath and walked into the room.

The nightmare I had been remembering faded to an overlay on the room as it was now. Like an empty stage after the last act. I ran my hand through my hair. It was stifling hot so I turned on the overhead fan and opened the window. That window, and the dying palm. How different a murder scene was when the victim was someone you loved.

I had come back here thinking I could be more objective now that the body was removed. I had been wrong. Sure the body was gone, and the blood had been washed away. If you didn't know what had caused the stains on the wall; if you didn't know they had probably just turned the mattress over and slipped on a new cover; if you didn't know someone's face had been blown all over the room; if you didn't know Antiay. If you didn't know, if you didn't know, if you didn't fucking know....

I wiped the sweat from my face. Too hot. I looked up to see if the fan was turning. It was, but slowly. I stared at it for a moment—not the fan really, but the ceiling. There was a hole in it. A small hole the size of my little finger. I shut off the fan and pulled the bed over to stand on. Using the screwdriver blade of my Swiss Army knife, I enlarged the hole until, sure enough, a hunk of lead dropped into my hand. It was misshapen, but definitely came from a .44 magnum handgun. I'd studied forensics—a lot of it in the field. I examined the fan blades and found a slight nick in the leading edge of one. The bullet had almost gone cleanly between the turning blades. I looked at the wall where the bloodstains were. The bullet hole there had been crudely filled with a patching compound. Maybe the other bullet was still in there, maybe they'd dug it out. It didn't matter. Two shots had definitely been fired.

That meant there had been a struggle. Antiay...and a man... someone strong enough to overpower her...she had tried to take the gun...she grabbed him by the wrist and forced the gun upward...first shot... he won the struggle...forced her to lie face down on the bed...she lifted her head to scream and...Jesus, oh shit, he shot her....

I stumbled to the window and leaned over, dizzy and almost sick again. I had seen the whole thing now and it was as real as if I'd been there. Who had killed her, damn it? Was it someone she knew? If so, why was she meeting him?

Or maybe he surprised her. Maybe, maybe...oh baby, why? Why, damn it, why?

I didn't feel any closer to the why. Every answer I got just brought more questions. Shit. My thinking was getting muddled again. All tangled up in emotion. For a moment, when I'd found the other bullet, I'd been a crystal clear detective again and the murder scene had clicked on, like turning on your television in the middle of a movie. That's how I was used to working. But this time the facts kept getting mixed up with wishes and beliefs, and everything became distorted. I still had the feeling something was wrong with the scene, but I couldn't figure out what it was.

I put the bullet in my pocket, closed the window, brushed the dust off the bed and returned it to its place, closed the door and locked it. I heard the television at the front desk blaring way up here. The old man was hard of hearing. If another tenant had noticed the shots, they hadn't called the police. Otherwise, the city police would have been here. But it was *federales.* That meant they were already coming, or maybe the murderer himself had called them. But why? Did he have a connection with them and knew he could manipulate them? Probably. Still, something important was missing.

I dropped the key at the desk. The guy didn't even look up from the TV. I walked back to the Hog and examined it for scratches. Nothing. Great. I swung my leg over. Next stop—the morgue.

LA PAZ WAS A small town, crime-wise. At least, before I arrived. I couldn't help but feel that somehow I'd brought all of this with me. Guilt—the gift that lasts forever. A little bit goes a long way too.

The police didn't have enough murders on their hands to justify their own morgue. They sent what bodies they did stumble across out to a mortuary just on the edge of town, on the road to Cabo. Probably owned by the brother of somebody important. I tried not to think about the crime on the ride out there. Maybe if I just kept digging without trying to figure out Antiay—if I just let the pieces find their own places....

I listened to the rumble of the Harley and tried to imagine a jazz number to go with that sound. No, it was its own jazz number, and there was always the wind massaging my hair.

I parked at the mortuary and took out my electronic pocket translator. It was about the size of a small pocket calculator, but it functioned like a Spanish-English dictionary. With my translator, I just punched in the word in English and it came back in Spanish.

I wrote down the translated words and walked into the office of the mortuary. A pretty receptionist looked up from the desk. She smiled and said, "*Buenos días.*"

"*Buenos días,*" I replied, then looked down at my cheat sheet. "*Estoy mirando para el cuerpo de una mujer...and er—*"

I looked up at her to see if she was getting it, and she was trying not to laugh at me. She got embarrassed.

"I'm sorry," she said. "Do you speak English? You have an American accent."

"Yes, yes I do. Thank goodness. I'm afraid my Spanish isn't very good."

"Yes," she said. "You would like to find out about someone who has died?"

"Please. A German woman who was murdered a few days ago. Her name was Antiay Mielke."

"Are you a friend or a relative?"

"I was a very close friend, but I just returned to La Paz last night. It was very bad news to hear. Do you know anything about it?"

"Yes, of course. The case is very well-known. But the body is not here. Do you know where is the cemetery here in La Paz?"

"Yes. Then she is already buried? Can you tell me how to find the grave?"

"Yes. Just a moment please, I'll look it up right here."

She went to a file cabinet and opened it. I had heard they wasted no time getting people in the ground. They usually didn't embalm them because of the extra expense. Still I was surprised—without a family—and I didn't think they'd had time to go through a consulate.

"Here it is." She returned with a map. "I'm sorry but it isn't very well marked when you arrive there. But the entrance is here, and the grave is here. All the way back in the right-hand corner. You will have to look for it, but I'm sure you'll be able to find it. Her sister is having a very nice gravestone erected, but there is a temporary—"

"Who? Who did you say?" I felt like I'd been punched again. My voice actually squeaked.

"Her sister took care of the arrangements. Sir, are you all right?"

"She doesn't have a sister," I shouted.

Now she became nervous. "I'm sorry sir, but she had all of the necessary papers. Look, she signed here. Gretchen Mielke. She was very beautiful. You didn't know the sister?"

I tried to get control of myself. "No. I'm afraid not. I'm sorry, this is all such a shock."

"Of course. I understand." We were getting back on familiar territory now and she relaxed a bit. Grieving friends and relatives were probably never easy.

"Do you know where her sister is staying? I'd like to meet her. And I have some photographs she might like to see. It must be difficult for her, too."

"Of course. I remember exactly where she is staying. I've seen it myself. In the harbor. A very large white yacht called the *Southern Cross*. The owner must be very rich to own—sir you are feeling sick again? I'm sorry if—"

I *was* feeling sick. Still. Sicker and sicker. I didn't bother to explain my pale face. I felt the blood had drained, and I wasn't even out of the door before it came rushing back in a surge of anger that probably made my face glow red. I kicked the walk, I stomped on the sidewalk, and I almost kicked the Hog. I really wanted to kick myself a real good hard one in the ass.

"What in hell is going on?" I screamed. Keep digging, let the pieces fall into place, be objective, don't get emotionally involved. Blah, blah, blah. What an ass I was. What a stupid, dumb, innocent ass. I should have stayed on the farm.

I smacked myself in the head one last time. A little too hard. I looked up and saw the receptionist staring at me like I was some madman who'd wandered into her neighborhood McDonald's with a machine gun. Except I was in La Paz and they didn't have a McDonald's yet. I laughed. It wouldn't be long now. They had liars, murders, drugs, gambling, corruption. Coming soon to a neighborhood near you would be Ronny McDonald with Big Macs for all.

The Hog rumbled. I waited a minute, then roared away from the house of the dead. Okay Mr. Gross Man, ready or not—here I come.

Chapter Nine

AFTER A COUPLE minutes I realized I was weaving through traffic faster than I should be, and I forced myself to slow down. There was no hurry. Grossman wasn't going anywhere. And if he did, I'd follow him to hell if I had to. It was time to meet this man I'd been hearing so many wonderful things about. After all, it wasn't fair to judge a person solely on gossip.

I shifted down and waited for the car in front of me to make whatever move his slow speed indicated he was considering. The car was loaded with kids and they were all staring out of the back window at me and the bike like I might be some kind of rock star. The Hog always attracted a lot of attention, I guess because they didn't see many of them down here. The car load of brothers and sisters all waved as their dad finally made his turn.

I waved back. Sisters. Why hadn't Antiay told me about her? Maybe the sister—what was her name—Gretchen? Maybe she had just flown in from Germany or something. Had there been time for that? Barely. I hadn't looked at the date of the burial. Another slip-up. I was getting damned near incompetent.

And she was staying on the *Southern Cross*. Why? She must know Grossman. What had the surfer kid said? That Victor bragged about having a rich German girlfriend on a big yacht? There was no denying Antiay and Victor had been close at one time. The photograph the governor had—

"Damn!" I said, swerving away from the carload of kids whose father had suddenly decided he wanted to drive where I was. Luckily there was room between him and the cattle truck in the next lane. I gunned the Hog and slipped between them, barely. *Whew! Pay attention to the traffic, Rick.*

I thought about going home for the cannon, but decided against it and turned right on *Cinco de Febrero*, heading down toward the Malecón. I didn't know for sure how I'd get out to the *Southern Cross*. I thought I might be able to catch a ride with one of the cruising sailors who beach their dinghies in front of the *Los Arcos* Hotel when they come in for supplies. If not, I could always borrow Hal's dingy.

I rounded the curve at Carlos and Charley's Restaurant on the beach, where the Malecón starts, and looked for the *Southern Cross*. At first I thought there was something wrong with my eyes—I'd just seen it a few hours ago. I searched the bay again and of course it wasn't there. You couldn't miss a yacht that big in this harbor. Grossman had slipped away. Damn.

Maybe I'd have to follow him to hell after all. I pulled onto the municipal pier hoping to find someone who could tell me where the *Southern Cross* was headed. I was in luck. Coming up the ramp from the Port Captain's boats was one of his men. I parked the Hog in his path, took out the equivalent of twenty dollars in pesos, and waited. It was a pretty good bribe for a small piece of information that was probably public knowledge anyway. But I didn't want to take any chances.

"*Buenos días, Señor,*" I said with my best I'm-a-tourist smile.

"*Buenos días,*" he replied, looking the Hog over.

"*Perdón Señor, pero necesito saber a dónde fue el yate Southern Cross? El dueño es mi amigo y necesito traerle un mensaje.*" I didn't know if I'd said it all right so I held the pesos up to him, and he took it with a blink. Hooked 'em. Great.

"*Su amigo se fue a* Cabo San Lucas."

"Cabo San Lucas? Damn!"

"*Pero va a parar a* Pichilingue *para combustibles y provisiones.*"

"Pichilingue? *La puerto nueva?*"

"*Sí. Para diesel.*"

"*Bueno. Muchas Gracias. Muy amable.*"

I was in luck. The *Southern Cross* was headed for Cabo San Lucas, but they had to stop at the new port dock in Pichilingue to take on fuel and supplies.

I had last seen them around 1:30 p.m. this afternoon. Even if they left right away, it would have taken them quite a while to get there and dock. That meant it would be well into the evening, at the earliest, before they could leave. These things take time in Mexico, and once in a while it works to your advantage.

I wheeled the Hog around and headed down the *Malecón* toward Pichilingue, glancing at my reflection in the left-hand rear-view mirror. *Mmmm*, still a little rough-looking. I hoped my date wouldn't mind.

The traffic was clear as I rode the highway toward Pichilingue. If only my head was. But the confusion in there would have made the morning commute in Mexico City look like a country drive.

I tried to forget it and glanced out at the Bay. The highway is cut through the red rock hills overlooking the water, and the view is fantastic. It's a nice highway to nowhere and back. Pichilingue is La Paz's deepwater port and is north of La Paz about seven miles. The inner harbor of La Paz is too shallow and shifting for deep-draft ships. So the freight comes into Pichilingue, including the huge truck and passenger-carrying ferries from the mainland.

The government had only recently opened up a huge new freight facility there, which is supposed to handle international freight, like container ships. That was the pier where the *Southern Cross* would be tied up.

Beyond Pichilingue the highway turned into a blacktop road which continued on to the end of the peninsula, ending at a beautiful, mile-long, half-moon, sandy beach called *Tecolote*, which means owl. That stretch of road had recently been blacktopped so a tourist complex was sure to follow. Too bad, because it was La Paz's favorite beach in the summer.

It wasn't quite sundown yet, so halfway to Pichilingue, I pulled into the *La Concha* Hotel to have a drink and watch the sunset. I didn't really have a plan for when I reached the *Southern Cross*, but darkness would give me a few more options in case I saw an opportunity to sneak aboard rather than announce myself.

I parked the Hog, and walked through the Hotel lobby and out to the pool bar where I ordered myself a tall *Cuba Libre*. A few couples sat around the pool, but I ignored them and took my drink down to the beach.

The *La Concha* has the best location of any hotel in La Paz. It's away from the town so it's very peaceful and the beach faces the world-famous sunsets, as all of La Paz does. I took off my shoes and socks, dug my toes into the sand, and waited for the sky to paint my heart a good one,

But if I thought I would find peace, even for a few moments, I was wrong. The day's events wouldn't let go, and I found myself tracing a circle in the sand. Then, spokes connecting to a hub, and in my mind, in the center, was Antiay's dead body. Wherever a spoke led I found a connection to Grossman. The Mafia—Grossman. The drug cartels—Grossman. White and the DEA—Grossman. The governor's son—Grossman. The gambling license—Grossman. Antiay's sister—Grossman again.

Now, in my mind, it all shifted and Grossman became the hub in the wheel, and Antiay's death just one of the spokes. Was that it? Was the bullet that blasted her into eternity just incidental somehow. Just a trivial sidebar to a powerful man's daily news? Was it possible her death had no meaning? That it wasn't a central event in the climactic scene?

I knew, from my own experience, that was usually the case with murder. These things weren't planned, they just sort of happened in the course of events, like car accidents. *Bam! Bam!* Oops! Usually, but not always. There were times when murder was the central theme and all else that passed were tracks in the sand.

I kicked out the wheel I'd drawn. For me it didn't matter. Antiay was the center and if a line led to Grossman, he was incidental. As the sun set and the sky turned to red, I pictured a faceless Grossman with my hands around his neck squeezing, squeezing, until the glass shattered and I looked down at the blood flowing from my left forefinger. I checked out the cut—it wasn't bad and there were no others. Lucky again.

I picked up the bits of glass in the sand. It was getting dark, and I hoped I'd got it all. I had the big pieces at least. After depositing the glass in a trashcan I tore off part of the handkerchief I carried only for such occasions, and wrapped it around my finger. Then I made my way to the taxi stand in front of the hotel and got in a cab. Somehow, back there on the beach, my subconscious mind was making rational decisions while my conscious mind was ranting and raving. For all I knew I might be going on a long cruise tonight, and the Hog would be safe here in the parking lot of the *La Concha*.

I told the driver where I wanted to go. As he drove, I tore another strip from my handkerchief, and assisting Dr. Hand with my teeth, tied it in a knot around the first bandage. It would have to do. Possibly it was only the first of many wounds this night would bring. Hopefully, not all mine.

I told the taxi driver to stop behind a small hill hiding us from the *Southern Cross*, and gave the driver an extra tip to turn around there in the road. Then I climbed the hill for a vantage point from which I hoped to form a plan of attack. I still hadn't decided against the direct approach. I could say I was a friend of Gretchen's dead sister and could we commiserate? That wasn't far from the truth. Sure I wanted to check out Grossman's operation, but I also wanted to talk to Antiay's sister. Maybe she could clear up some of the questions I had. Maybe she even had some ideas of her own about why Antiay was murdered. Maybe we would just cry on each other's shoulder.

Sure enough, when I reached the crest of the hill a brilliant plan took on a life of its own. Below me was the *Southern Cross* tied to the pier, and on the pier were three semi-trailer trucks being emptied of various sized crates, which were then on-loaded onto the huge yacht. I knew it was risky, but I wanted a look at those crates if possible. One thing was certain—those weren't your ordinary supplies. They didn't package lettuce and onions in wooden crates.

I stumbled three times getting back down to the road. The moon wasn't up yet and it had become dark. Once on the road I made my way in the shadows until I was hidden behind the warehouse. There didn't seem to be any guards around, at least that I could make out. There was a lot of open space between me and the semis, and if anyone was watching from the bridge of the *Southern Cross*, they could certainly see that area.

I decided to walk across the open space as if I was part of the crew gone to take a leak or something. I had a good tan. Assuming my best hourly-wage slouch, I sauntered over to the trucks. So far, so good. Now I made my way along the side of the trailer parked farthest away from the yacht, and watched the crew working the freight. There were only three of them, with one lift truck, so it was slow-going. And they were working on the trailer farthest away from me. The door of the trailer nearest me was open and all I had to do was wait until the crew's backs were turned, and hoist myself inside. Then I could examine the crates at my leisure. Hot dog!

I crouched down and waited my chance. Now! I sprang up and— jumped a foot in the air as a big hand clamped itself on my shoulder, scaring the shit out of me. Looking around, I prepared myself for a karate stance that might cover the fact I'd just been startled out of my wits, but the other big hand was holding a 9-MM automatic. I'd just have to look jumpy. Under the circumstances, it was understandable. Big Hand nodded for me to move toward the yacht.

Once we'd cleared the trucks I looked back again. Big Hand nodded toward the gangplank. I trooped along like a tourist caught snapping pictures of a military facility, earnest in my innocence. By his demeanor, Big Hand demonstrated he could care less, much less care at all. He was at least 6'7", which meant he was probably always banging his head on board the *Southern Cross*, and he weighed at least three hundred pounds, none of which seemed to be fat. For a huge man he was very athletic, because he'd managed to sneak up behind me and that hadn't often been done before. You had to admire a worthy opponent, and under different circumstances I'd have bought him a beer. Some other time. The game was just beginning.

"Come aboard Mr. Sage, come aboard," a self-assured, authoritative voice said from somewhere out of sight above as we reached the gangplank. "Bobby, I don't think we'll need the armament. Mr. Sage has come to visit us, and we must treat him like a guest. All private investigators are curious animals. We must expect it. Welcome Mr. Sage, welcome."

I actually laughed when he called Big Hand, Bobby. I looked back but little Bobby didn't even chuckle. Then I climbed the gangplank stairs with a smile. And why not? Waiting for me there at the top, at last, was

Jurgen Grossman. He was grinning from ear to ear—which was quite a distance. Unlike Bobby, Grossman lived up to his name. A very gross man. Five foot about seven inches tall and two hundred and fifty pounds gross, none of which appeared to be muscle. He was dressed all in white, including his punk style crew cut. He looked like the Pillsbury Doughboy's bad brother.

He extended a dumpling hand and we shook. His handshake revealed a deceptive strength. Under the fat there must be some muscle after all. "I'm glad to meet you," he said. "I've been hearing so much about you."

"Did they tell you I love your cookies?" I said with a grin.

"No, I'm afraid not. But they did warn me about your strange sense of humor. Something about a wise guy. Whatever that means."

"I'm afraid I can't argue with that."

"We meet at last. Come in. Make yourself at home."

He led the way into the main salon. It was twice as large as most living rooms and contained several easy chairs, sofas, an entertainment center, a bar and a large rectangular dining table.

"Please have a seat." He motioned toward the leather and chrome captain's chairs at the bar, and he slipped behind it. Little Bobby took a position just behind me. The automatic had disappeared into a pocket and he stood there at a military parade rest with his hands clasped in front of him.

"What would you like to drink, Mr. Sage?"

"A *Cuba Libre*, dark."

He mixed the drink and set it in front of me. "One *Cuba Libre*, dark. Tell me, to what do we owe the pleasure of this visit?"

I watched as he poured himself a couple of fingers of Scotch. "Didn't White tell you? You were obviously expecting me."

He raised his glass, stared into my eyes and said, "*Salud!*"

He had very pale, almost colorless blue eyes, eyes without emotion, cunning animal eyes that flickered when I didn't answer his toast. He hesitated, then drank, and set his glass down. "It's true, I was expecting you. That's why I sent Bobby out to invite you aboard. Unfortunately, Bobby is unable to speak—due to an encounter with a knife a couple of years ago. I'm sorry if he surprised you." A slight smile appeared on his lips.

"That's all right. I got curious about those wooden crates that are being loaded onboard. I've heard quite a lot about your various enterprises. I've been around the military, and those crates remind me of the way weapons are packaged."

"Oh, my, I was warned you have an overactive imagination. I'm afraid there's nothing so romantic as military armaments in those crates. Some of them are big enough to be coffins, but does that mean they must contain corpses? No, no, of course not. Any corpses, we simply throw overboard once we're at sea." He gave me another of his little grins, and winked. "My, my, we've gone off on quite a tangent haven't we? You were about to tell me why you are here?"

"I wasn't about to tell you anything, Sleazeball." Hey bingo! The zombie eyes really flickered that time. "I'm investigating the murder of a very close friend. And every time I ask questions, your name seems to pop up. You're acquiring a very nasty reputation. Gunrunning, gambling, drugs, and murder. I want to know what you know about Antiay Mielke's death. And if I don't get a satisfactory answer, I'm going to make you my hobby. I don't think you'd like the publicity I think I can generate for you. Sleazeballs like you usually prefer operating underneath a slimy rock."

The doughboy's eyes flickered again and I knew they were contemplating death. Mine. It only took an instant for him to decide, and then he smiled once again, a signal I was sure was meant for Bobby. Grossman evidently wasn't a gambler and I was an unknown quantity. He'd wait. He had a lot of confidence.

"You needn't get so personal Mr. Sage. Still, I understand, you've lost someone you were close to. I'm sorry, but I don't know who her murderer is. It is my understanding that the police considered you a strong suspect." He held up his hand to quiet me. "However, I believe you are a stubborn man, and you are right about one thing. I don't like undue publicity. My clients are very sensitive to invasions of privacy, shall we say? Perhaps we could reach an agreement. I am quite wealthy, and private investigators, I'm quite sure, are not. Would, say, a fifty thousand dollar fee insure my privacy?"

I love it when they offer a bribe. "There are some things money can't buy. I told you, you give me the murderer and I'll forget about your sleazy endeavors. I don't care what you do, but I'm going to find out who killed Antiay. If you want me to lay off, you'll have to hand him over. Do we understand each other?"

"I think we do Mr. Sage. I think we do. But you're not the only one interested in Antiay Mielke's murderer. There's someone I want you to meet. Bobby."

Bobby disappeared around the corner and down the forward passageway. I sipped my drink and waited. In a minute he returned, nodded to Grossman, and took up his station behind me. I was taking another sip from my drink when she entered the room—the glass slipped from my fingers and tumbled to the floor. "Antiay," I mumbled.

"Antiay—" I became dizzy as I reached out to touch her, like you would a ghost. The room whirled as the doughboy cackled.

"Mr. Sage, you didn't know? You didn't know? You look like you've seen a ghost. But this isn't Antiay—she's dead. It's true I'm afraid. This is her twin sister, Gretchen. Identical twins, they were. Gretchen, meet Rick Sage, the man they say murdered your sister."

It wasn't all registering because standing in front of me was Antiay and words meant nothing, but then the ghost spit in my face and fingernails clawed at my cheek.

"Murderer!" she screamed. "Murderer!"

I looked away and saw Grossman grinning like a hangman. I whirled and kicked into Bobby's crotch. He'd been watching the sideshow and I caught him by surprise. As he went down, I kicked him again, this time up beside the head. That seemed to slow him down, so I turned my attention back to Grossman. I'd surprised him too, so I reached over the bar and squeezed his fat doughboy neck between my two hands. He reached back, grabbing me by the throat, and we were locked in a death struggle.

His pale face turned red, then redder as I squeezed his neck tighter, like you do the frosting decorator on Christmas cookies. I could feel his thumbs gouging into my windpipe, but that only made me squeeze harder. I was going for a nice purple color, when I caught movement out of the corner of my eye. I looked in time to see the Antiay look-alike swing a bottle at my head. I was fascinated by the sight and read the label, like in slow motion, as it crashed into my forehead. The label of the Bacardi Añejo translated itself into a drumming mantra accompanying my long fall into night: "Dark rum...rum...rum...rum...rum..."

Chapter Ten

I WAS AWAKE before I opened my eyes. I didn't want to wake up, but somebody was banging on a very big drum somewhere inside my head and I couldn't get back to sleep. The smell of alcohol was strong. Did that mean I'd been to a party? Was that why my head was throbbing so hard it made me feel like puking? I couldn't remember. I didn't think I wanted to, either. I rolled over and waited for sleep to return. The floor was very hard but that was okay. I just wanted to sleep.

"Sage." I heard my name being called through a very thick fog. I knew I'd been asleep for a long while because this time I wanted to wake up. The drums were still beating inside my head, but they were beating out a message that said something was wrong. "Sage," again, only this time from much closer. A hard object struck me in the back and my eyes flew open.

"Oh no, not again," I mumbled. I looked at the other bodies sprawled around. I couldn't tell if they were the same prisoners, but this was definitely the same cell.

"Sage, get up!" Something struck me in the back again. I was awake now, and I realized someone was kicking me. I rolled away and looked up. I'd been sleeping next to the bars and someone on the outside was kicking me awake.

"Stand up Sage!"

"White, you bastard!"

"Stand up, bum!"

Bracing myself with the bars I did as he said. Not because he said to, but because I wanted to look him level in the eyes and let him know how lucky he should feel to have these bars between us. And maybe he'd fuck up and get too close—

"Okay, take it," I heard White say, as the flash of a camera blinded me, making the drums surge again.

"Shit!"

"You're in it deep, Sage."

The photographer and the guard went away, leaving White standing there grinning at me.

"What did you say, White?" He moved a little closer but stopped just out of range.

"I said you're standing in deep shit. This is the second time in less than a week you've been picked up for public drunkenness. These people frown on that kind of thing. I wouldn't be surprised if they left you in here for awhile. On the other hand, maybe they'll revoke your visa and deport you. I think I'll encourage them to do all of the above. Somehow, I feel sure you're going to be out of my hair for awhile. Even if you get out of here, your credibility is about zero. Yes sir, you're worth about as much right now as a three-day-old dog turd."

He turned and walked away, laughing. I didn't say anything. My head wasn't in any shape for snappy repartee. Besides, I wasn't in a position to brag. They'd caught me twice in the same trap and that was embarrassing. I was sure having the photographer take my picture meant they were going to play it up in the newspapers. "Boyfriend of suicide victim arrested for second time for public drunkenness" or some similar headline. There wasn't much I could do but wait for Freddy or Pepe to read about it in the papers. I didn't know if they could get me out a second time, but they were my only hope.

I sat back down, then laid down. Suddenly I was very tired again. I wasn't going anywhere so I might as well get some sleep, if I could.

"*Señor Sage.*" I looked at my watch. It was only ten to eleven and already I was popular.

"*¡Señor Sage!*" Now the guard sounded impatient. I stood up as he unlocked the cell door. "*¡Ven!*" he said. That means come, and after I stepped out he relocked the cage and led me down the hall. He was very trusting with his back turned to me. Evidently I wasn't considered dangerous. That was a bad mistake. I hadn't made my own mind up yet—I was a little slow this morning. I had to get out of here somehow because I had places to be and people to see. Like Gretchen for instance. And there was the deadline on the gambling license. Once the governor was forced to choose a side, our deal would be off and things would get much tougher for me. They were bad enough now. On the other hand, being an escapee from the law wasn't going to make things any easier either. No, they were right—I wasn't dangerous. I'd just have to go with the flow, for now.

He led me through two more doors and down two more passages before he stopped beside a third door and motioned for me to enter.

I did. It was a small interrogation room. I closed the door behind me. Seated behind a table was a well-dressed lawyer type who stood up and extended his hand when I entered. "Mr. Sage." We shook hands. "My name is Alfredo Abaroa. I'm the chief prosecutor here. Have a seat please."

We both sat down as my spirits raised. He was Pepe's friend—the same guy who'd released the surfer kid from jail. "Thanks for your help on that other matter," I said, "I wanted to thank you, but I hoped it would be under better circumstances."

"Yes, it seems your method of investigation is a bit unusual. The bad guys are the ones who are supposed to end up in jail."

We both laughed. "Yeah, you're right. I do seem to be getting things backwards. But it's all part of the plan."

"Let's hope so."

"How did you find out I was in here so fast? I was sure they were going to misplace the paperwork."

"This is my territory. I am informed immediately if something unusual is happening. Your government's DEA seems to have a rather simplistic understanding of our system."

"They have a very simplistic view of the world."

"I suppose that goes with the territory, as they say in the North. Well then, perhaps it is up to the rest of us to take a larger view of things. I'm going to have you released, but since this is your second time getting arrested in less than a week, and because of the publicity, we need to follow the rules. In other words, for me to release you, you must confess to your crime and be assessed a small fine. It would be too complicated and time consuming if you were to insist on your innocence. I assume you wish to be released as soon as possible?"

"Yes, yes of course. I understand completely. What's the procedure?"

"You will be taken from here and brought before a judge. It has all been arranged. You will sign in various places, pay the fine, and be released. You have the necessary money amongst your property. We checked. In less than thirty minutes you will be a free man again."

"Thanks. Thanks for sticking your neck out for me."

"It's nothing. Pepe Acosta believes in you and I believe in Pepe. Also, I spent some time in the United States and some people there helped me out a few times. Maybe I'm just passing it on—repaying an old debt."

"I'll try to pass it on to someone else. I thought you might have lived up North for a while. Your English is almost perfect. Most of us don't speak it that well. Where did you study?"

"I received my law degree from Harvard. My father wanted me to become President of Mexico. Unfortunately, I didn't like living in Mexico City. I missed La Paz. So, I came home. It worked out well—my father missed me, too."

"Lucky for me and La Paz."

He stood up and we shook hands.

"Try to stay out of jail. You know what they say—three strikes and you're out."

"I won't be back. I'm getting very close to some answers in this case and it's beginning to make some powerful people nervous. I don't think they'll try this old trick again. It's getting to the point where it's me or them."

"Good luck, and be careful. If there's anything more I can do be sure to call on me. Here's my card."

I took the card, we shook hands again, and he went to the door and opened it. He said something in Spanish to the guard, then he walked away. Twenty minutes later, I was on the street hailing a taxi. Who said they don't have a revolving door justice system? Not that I'm complaining.

I had the cabby drop me off at the *La Concha* Hotel and I picked up the Hog. I didn't want to be seen, if possible, so I took back streets to my place. The longer they thought I was still in jail, the better. It meant surprise would be on my side. I figured they wouldn't be watching my place, because they thought they knew where I was. I was right. The street was empty and I drove right through the gate and parked inside the wall, underneath the bougainvillea.

So far so good. Thanks to Guille, the house was all Humpty Dumptied back together again. Her tip was going to be enormous, and she deserved every peso of it.

In spite of the heat, I took a very long, hot shower. I let it run for a long time on the back of my neck. Then I shut off the hot water and stood under the cold for an equal amount of time. When I finally got out, I was feeling almost human again, although the headache drums were following me closer than shadows in the jungle. I popped three Percodans, shaved, toothbrushed, and put a nickel in Mr. Coffee. Then I sat down naked, under the fan by the telephone, sipping the hot java.

I picked up the phone and dialed Freddy's number. He answered.

"It's Rick."

"I was beginning to worry about you, *mi amigo*."

"I spent the night tumbling around inside one of those front-loading washing machines, but other than that I'm fine."

"You did what?"

"Never mind, I'm okay. Say Freddy, can you do something for me?"

"Yeah, no problem. Do I need a vest that is bullet proof?"

"No, I hope not. But it is a little sensitive. I need to know if there is someone in town from Las Vegas, Nevada. Someone, maybe Italian, who is associated with that Hotel over on the Mogote, the...what's it called...*La*

Mision."

"*Sí, sí* that's it, *La Mision. Qué pasa?*"

"I don't know Freddy. It's just a hunch. I met our Mr. Grossman yesterday—the guy on the *Southern Cross*. He's a crook all right. Got his chubby little fingers in all kinds of illegal and semi-legal pies. I got very close to him—I was squeezing on his fat neck and he was doing the same to mine. Trouble is, I realized I wanted to choke him to death worse than he wanted to kill me. He's not an impulse killer. He plans everything out. He may be responsible for Antiay's death, or he may just know who did it, and why. But something is missing. Do you understand?"

"You're not making a lot of sense. You think Grossman isn't the murderer because he didn't choke on your neck hard enough?"

"Something like that. I said it was just a hunch. I've made mistakes before. That's all right if it doesn't get you killed. I solved a case one time by making nothing but mistakes. The more mistakes I made, the closer it took me to the real killer. By accident. I'll tell you about it sometime. Anyway, the Mafia's involved in this gambling deal—trying to get a casino license for the *La Mision* Hotel. I just wonder if they didn't send someone to La Paz without telling Grossman. A sort of back-up. That's the way they operate. I don't know, but if you could check around I'd appreciate it."

"Sure Rick. If there's someone like that in town, I should be able to find him. You *gringos* stand out like big thumbs in La Paz."

"Sore thumbs, Freddy."

"Okay, those, too. Anything else? Where should I contact you?"

"I don't think there's anything else right now. I'll call you. I've got a date with a beautiful woman so I'll be out of touch"

"All right, *amigo*, it's good—get back in the saddle. That's what I'd do."

"I know, Freddy. Talk to you later."

"Yeah man, have one for me. *Hasta luego.*"

"*Hasta luego.*" I hung up the phone and thought about Antiay and her sister Gretchen. I planned to go to Cabo San Lucas, locate the *Southern Cross*, and one way or another, I'd have my say. Gretchen would have to hear me out. When I saw her yesterday she looked exactly like Antiay. Were they really so much alike? I had heard of identical twins whose personalities were so alike that even when they hadn't seen each other for years, they still picked out identical clothes. I had a feeling these two sisters had at least a few differences. And I needed to remind myself that she wasn't Antiay. But the memory of the hatred Gretchen had shown toward me hurt far worse than the lump she'd left on my head. I had to convince her of my innocence, and make her examine what she had heard on Grossman's boat that might give me a clue to the real murderer. At least I had to try.

I made myself a peanut butter and honey sandwich, and washed it down with another cup of coffee. Then I opened a Corona from the fridge and chugged half of it, finally washing the last of the peanut butter off the roof of my mouth. Percodans, coffee, and beer—some combination for a long ride after a concussion. The thing about a motorcycle is you have lots of room on your side of the road if you weave a bit. I picked out the red bowling shirt, the one that said 'Frank' over the pocket. The logo across the back read, "Harley Lanes – Have a ball in Hell!" And there was a picture of a guy on a motorcycle throwing a flaming bowling ball.

I dug the cannon out of the hole along with two clips and the belt holster. Then I wrapped them up in my leather jacket, grabbed an extra shirt, my shaving kit and the travel alarm clock, and went out to the Hog. I packed everything in the saddlebags, then checked the canteen I always carried. It was full. After a couple of minutes warm-up, I hit the road for Cabo San Lucas.

For a change I kept my speed down to a nice calm fifty-five miles per hour. It was another beautiful day in Baja, and I was in no hurry. I'd had enough excitement lately, and speed seemed rather tame in comparison. Although the road made me feel better, I was still pretty shaky and tired. And I wasn't in any hurry. I'd wanted to get out of town fast, before I ran into White or one of his gang. But now that I was on the road, I had lots of time to lean on the grips and contemplate the universe, and the evil deed of murder. I didn't need to get to Cabo much before dark, and it was only 2:30 p.m. now.

As the cactus rushed past, I got the feeling they were moving and I was sitting still. An army of cactus marching on La Paz. It was an illusion of course, but maybe it would make a good B-movie science fiction plot.

Illusion. I'd had plenty of that lately. A stranger in Antiay's body coming at me like something out of *The Night of the Living Dead.* I couldn't remember anymore what Antiay's loving face had looked like. The memory had been erased by a blonde corpse without a face, a grinning photograph, and the attack of Gretchen screaming, "Murderer." And this twin sister seemed to be allied somehow with Grossman, whom I suspected of being involved in Antiay's death.

The cactus marched on to the rumble of the Harley engine, and I thought about Grossman. I'd told Freddy I didn't think Grossman was the murderer, but I wasn't sure. Nothing was as it seemed. Like Alice in Wonderland, I couldn't be sure of anything except that he hadn't actually pulled the trigger himself. He'd have someone like Bobby do it. But there was something wrong with that scenario. If Grossman had murdered Antiay...there were pieces missing from the puzzle. He had said he threw dead bodies overboard. It sounded like a crude joke, but if he did have someone murdered, that was more his style.

I kept forgetting, though. Maybe whoever had shot Antiay hadn't planned to do it. That left everyone in the picture. Even her sister. Could Gretchen have been acting when she called me a murderer? I didn't know. I was in shock at seeing her. I thought she was Antiay, and expected her to throw herself into my arms. I hadn't been in any condition to pay attention to small details.

It was a hunch, but I felt all the players hadn't appeared yet. Maybe Freddy would find something. The Mafia seldom left things to chance. Grossman wasn't really their man. It only made sense they would have someone here to—

Damn fool! A pick-up came at me weaving all over the road—only a few hundred yards away and a split second to decide if I could maneuver around him. I hit the brakes and skidded sideways, but got it under control. My speed dropped down to maybe fifteen miles per hour, but the pick-up almost on top of me as he swerved right at me. I had no choice and left the highway. Now it was ride 'em cowboy—dust flying and the Hog taking at least two small jumps—and my feet flying off the pegs and my butt bouncing higher than my head, but somehow she kept upright until I came back down in the seat with my left foot finding the rear brake. Then she hit the sand and the front wheel stopped dead while the back wanted to keep going. She jackknifed on top of me, on my left leg, and I lay pinned in the sand. I reached up and cut the engine and tried to pull myself out from under her.

Luckily we landed in soft sand, and after a moment I was able to pull out my leg. I stood up and it seemed okay; at least nothing was broken or bleeding.

The most important thing was to try to get the Hog upright as soon as possible, before the vital fluids ran out of her. I sat down in the sand with my back next to her and my heels dug in. Then I pushed against her twelve hundred pounds and she moved, but my right foot lost traction and she settled back down.

I dug in again and this time the Hog rose slowly with me as I steadied her upright. I rested there for a moment surveying the damage. There didn't seem to be much. The left mirror was pushed out of whack and there was some sand and dry weeds on the left side of the engine. I couldn't see a scratch on the paint, so I relaxed a bit.

I looked back at the route I'd taken after leaving the road and realized just how lucky I was. There was no shoulder off the highway, as usual in Baja. Instead there was a slight incline of packed gravel descending to a depth of about five feet below the level of the highway. I saw the first bump I'd felt was when we left the highway, and the second was a small rut at the bottom of the incline just before the soft sand of the arroyo run-off we'd landed in. If I'd lost it on the incline there probably would have been more damage. And I'd just missed a large rock at the bottom.

I started to swear, but caught myself and thanked the gods instead. If I didn't know better I would have thought someone up there was looking out for me. If it was only the blind fates, they deserved thanks. Any detective needs a guardian angel to survive. I just wished I could get mine to come to the horse track with me. Maybe that's pushing my luck. Probably why I couldn't win.

The immediate problem was how to get the Hog back on the road. She was stuck smack dab in the middle of very soft sand.

It took a lot of work, but gradually, by lifting and dragging first one end and then the other, I got the front wheel back on solid ground. Then I started her up and by idling in first gear and pushing at the same time, I finally worked her out of the sand, up the incline, and back on the highway.

It had been about a half an hour since I'd left the road, and I wondered if I could catch the bastard in the pick-up. I decided not. I was only about a half an hour out of La Paz, and he'd be lost in the crowd. It was hard to let him go, but I decided I didn't have a choice. I cleaned off the Hog, checked everything out, and finally headed toward Cabo again.

Once I was on the road and the bike checked out okay, I started thinking about the accident. Was it really an accident? Maybe the guy was drunk, or maybe he was just trying to look that way. For that matter, I didn't even know for sure if it was a guy. Could have been a woman—I didn't get a close look. I had an image of a baseball cap and white teeth inside a grinning mouth. The grin was like a skull grin, like death's grin, and I wasn't sure that I hadn't just imagined it. But in my mind I could see a stop-action shot where I looked through the windshield of that pick-up, and death was at the wheel wearing a baseball cap.

I decided I'd better keep that to myself. But the other part, the feeling that whoever was driving was actually trying to run me off the road—that was real. Of course it could have been a crazy drunk, or just a crazy person. They had them down here, too. Not in the quantity or quality of Los Angeles crazies—that was a special pressure cooker recipe. But there were a few *loco* people in Baja.

Maybe I was being paranoid, but the drunk or crazy angle seemed too much like coincidence. There were people who'd like to see me out of the way. Maybe they'd found out I'd been released from jail. It wouldn't be hard for them to guess I'd head for Cabo San Lucas, following the *Southern Cross*. Several vehicles had passed me on the highway, and one of them was similar to the pick-up that had run me off the road. I hadn't paid much attention to them though, because I'd been thinking about the case.

It really didn't matter in the end whether it had been an accident or attempted murder. If it was the latter, it had failed. I was very much alive and still on track. All they'd managed to do was give me was a sore leg and another grudge for when I finally caught up with them.

I decided to take a break from thinking about it. I opened the cassette box and pulled out my favorite EAGLES' tape: *The Hotel California*. That hotel is in Todos Santos, a small town down the road another half an hour, at this speed. The Hotel California was still there and, if anything, was in better shape than when the Eagles recorded the song about it. I intended to stop in for a beer or two, so I popped the tape in the deck, turned up full volume, and began to sing along. Out of key I'm sure because I couldn't hear myself over the bike's rumble and the powerful amplified speakers. But so what if I was out of tune? The turkey buzzards munching roadkill didn't seem to mind.

Chapter Eleven

I STOPPED AT the Hotel California in Todos Santos and had a late lunch and a couple of beers. The food was great and the hotel was interesting. It was a part of rock culture history, but what really made it nice, in fact the reason the song was even written, was the town of Todos Santos and its location.

Todos Santos is an oasis situated within a mile of the ocean. It has a fresh water spring and fertile soil. It straddles the two-lane highway to the cape, which used to be just a dirt road. The ocean beaches near Todos Santos are some of the finest sandy beaches in the world. You come out of the desert, over a hill, and there is a lush tropical oasis with a fine hotel and relatively prosperous people. Of course it's changed over the years— what hasn't? But I have a friend named Raymundo who was raised there, and to hear him tell it, Todos Santos, at that time, was one of the best places in the world to grow up in. I believe it.

I left Todos Santos just in time to catch the sunset out over the ocean, on a fifteen-mile stretch of highway where I could watch it as I rode along. It was a beautiful ride God had to have created especially for a Harley. By the time I reached Cabo San Lucas, I was in a great mood and almost didn't remember the reason I'd come. I felt so good I might have hugged the evil little doughboy, Grossman, if I'd encountered him.

Making my way to the beach near the *El Delfin* restaurant, I could see the *Southern Cross* riding at anchor. She was lit up like a Las Vegas casino. I sat down at one of the tables set up on the sandy beach, where I could watch the yacht, and ordered a *Cuba Libre*, dark. I could see the yacht's tender tied up alongside the gangway, so I assumed they were all aboard for dinner. If they were entertaining guests, which was likely considering they had made a special trip over here, then it made sense they would be aboard. I decided to watch and wait and see what happened. Hopefully they would come ashore for a round of the discos. That's what yachties did at night in Cabo. If not I would board her later—by stealth if possible, by force if necessary.

The waiter came back with the drink and I asked him about the *Southern Cross*. He didn't speak any English, however we managed to communicate in spite of my bad Spanish. I said I had met a woman from that yacht in La Paz, but I didn't know they would be here in Cabo. He

said they came here often, but only for two or three days at a time. I told
him I had met my friend at a disco and I hoped she'd be coming ashore
tonight. He asked if she was a very beautiful woman with blonde hair and
a fantastic body? He didn't actually say the word body, but he outlined the
appropriate curves and grinned with one eyebrow raised. We were doing a
lot of sign language to compensate for my lack of fluency. I said yes, there
could be no mistake—that was her. He laughed, and I asked him if he
knew her well. He sighed and said no, not well. She had swum ashore in
the afternoon, drank a margarita at that very table next to me, paid with
money he demonstrated she had removed from her swim top, and then she
swam away like a mermaid. He pulled a large denomination peso bill from
his shirt pocket and indicated it was the one she paid with. He said he
would keep it for luck, and kissed it with enthusiasm. I agreed it would
bring very good luck, and hoped I would be lucky enough to see her
tonight. He said it was possible because she had mentioned the discos
when he asked her if she liked Cabo San Lucas. I would be the lucky one,
he went on, if I should be fortunate enough to dance with such a beautiful
woman. I agreed, thanked him, and tipped him for the information.

Gretchen had another thing in common with Antiay besides their
looks. They were evidently both excellent swimmers. Antiay was the best
swimmer I had ever known. She could out-swim me by far, and I was no
slouch even though I'd learned my technique trying to keep from
drowning in a mill-pond near where I'd grown up.

Antiay and I had been at the beach one day, and I'd asked her where
she'd learned to swim so well. She was like a dolphin in the water. For an
instant her eyes sparkled. She said she had always loved the sea and when
she was a little girl she had dreamed of changing into a dolphin. She swam
whenever she could and at one time was training for the Olympic team
in—

She never finished her sentence and her eyes went sad. She got that
faraway look and said she was sorry, but she didn't wish to talk about it.
All that was a different time, she said, staring out over the water—another
life. "I never became a dolphin," she whispered, and we had hugged as
saltwater tears rolled down her cheeks.

I wiped mine away and ordered a drink. That had been another
lifetime, too. I just hoped that wherever she was now, there was a sea as
beautiful as the one before me, and she was a dolphin at last.

I meandered through a couple more drinks like that, until ten minutes
after ten when I saw the tender pull away from the *Southern Cross*, headed
for the inner harbor. I paid my bill and left, riding the Hog over the hill. I
knew they'd be tying up at the marina there and I found a spot where I

would be hidden from view. They must have called ahead from the yacht, because a taxicab was waiting for them as they came up the ramp from the dock. I could make out Gretchen and a Latino who appeared to be her date.

They got in the taxi and drove away. I followed at a reasonable distance. I didn't know if Gretchen knew about the Harley or not. It wasn't exactly the common, ordinary, low-key vehicle recommended in the Tailing Suspects chapter of the Detective's Handbook.

I really didn't need to tail them at all. I had guessed where they were going. Sure enough, the taxi pulled into the parking lot of the *Cabo-Wabo* nightclub. It was the hottest nightspot in Baja Sur. Partly owned by some U.S. rock star, it had that combination of star charisma and fad style that attracts the night crowd like lemmings to the sea.

Not that I was immune. I had been there with Antiay a few times. I liked to dance. What my aunt had saved on a swimming instructor she spent on forced dancing lessons. I put a curse on her for it at the time, but removed it a couple of years later when I discovered my expertise brought me in close contact with the hot young bodies of all the best-looking girls. It's one lesson I didn't forget. And Antiay was no exception. She had been an excellent dancer.

I didn't really care much for the crowd hanging out here. They were mostly tourists who fly down from places like Los Angeles, New York, and Chicago, packing superiority complexes that swell under the influence of alcohol, to enormous dimensions, making them seem like big-headed alien invaders from up Uranus. Maybe I'm being harsh. I hate to stereotype and I'm only talking maybe two percent. But a little bit of obnoxious goes a long way.

I held back until they were inside, then I parked the Hog in the shadows away from the mainstream of the parking lot, and waited. It would take awhile for them to get into the rhythm of the place and over the initial I-see-you-do-you-see-me routine. A couple of drinks, a couple of dances, and they'd be part of the crowd. Thirty minutes later I slipped inside.

Now I'm kind of big I guess, so it's not always easy for me to go unnoticed, even in a large group. But there were a lot of people in the *Cabo Wabo* on this particular night so I managed to slip into a dark corner near the bar. I saw Gretchen almost immediately. She was on the dance floor, and once again my gut felt like I'd been punched unexpectedly. The resemblance was remarkable, truly identical. She was wearing a tight black mini-dress that showed curves so much like Antiay's, I could drive them blindfolded.

The waiter came and I ordered a drink without taking my eyes off her. I tried hard to find differences. The enthusiasm of her dance was the only detail I could find that seemed different from Antiay. Gretchen seemed to be going through the motions—like she really wasn't interested. Not quite bored, but distracted. Maybe she didn't care for her partner. He was certainly doing everything he could to impress her. In fact he was trying too hard, and it was obvious. Well, that was his problem. It was good for me. If she wasn't romantically involved with this guy, then she was just entertaining. Which meant she might take the time to hear me out. Or she might attack, screaming murderer again, and I'd have to fight off her date and all of his relatives. It was a toss-up.

After a few minutes, they returned to their seats to quench the thirst they'd worked up.

Now what? I had no real plan other than to try to talk to her alone. I considered asking her to dance, but that seemed too confrontational. I had an idea what her reaction would be to seeing me. The lump on my head testified to it. I tried to be patient.

A plan formed as I watched them in conversation at their table. There was no holding hands or the excited laughter you expect from a couple in love, or lust. They seemed to be chatting formally, maybe about the decor or their respective tastes in music. If I was wrong and there was some romantic attachment, my plan might not work. But it was the only one I could think of.

Finally, he ordered another round of drinks and they headed for the dance floor.

I took out my wallet and removed the foil package from its compartment. Gretchen and her date were dancing on the far side of the crowded floor, and I could barely see them as I waited for their drinks to arrive.

A pharmacist friend of mine in the States supplied me with the foil packets, which contained just enough sedative that, combined with a few drinks, would put any ordinary person to sleep, or at least make them groggy. He had assured me it was safe as long as the person wasn't entirely drunk. Gretchen's date seemed very much in control. The packets had come in handy several times in my career and I always kept one with me.

When their drinks arrived at their table, I made my way over to it. I sat down as if I belonged there, and after a moment, poured the powder from the packet into his drink. I gave it a quick mix with my finger, and sat there a moment longer. I looked around, and reassured that no one had paid the slightest attention to me, I stood up and returned to my corner. Let the games begin.

They went on dancing for quite a while and I had to admit he was good. She, like Antiay, was also very good. I felt jealous watching them, in spite of my attempts to control it. I also felt anger. A lot of anger. Jealousy or anger—neither is a very satisfying emotion, and as I sat there, I grew disgusted with myself for playing the detective game. I wanted revenge and there were plenty of candidates around—all of them slime of one sort or another. If I was sure Grossman was involved, why didn't I just go out there and feed him and his henchman to the fishes? Why not? He was guilty of enough other crimes even if he wasn't responsible for taking Antiay from me. *Why not just do it?* But someone inside answered back. *Because that's murder*, the voice said. *Murder, remember?* The crime you've dedicated your life to fighting. If you take the easy way you must cross over, and when that happens you are one with them. All of them. You would be part of Antiay's brutal death—one with the monster who killed her.

The anger and jealousy passed, but the black hole of loneliness remained. In some ways I was no more than a robot now, programmed for a single purpose. Find the person who pulled the trigger, prove it, and make him pay the price. I wasn't after gun-runners, cocaine cartels, gamblers, or the Mafia. What I wanted was the person who pulled the trigger. If I didn't concentrate on that single deed, first and foremost, the world would become an infinite tangle of shared guilt. It wasn't my job to worry about whether Johnny Axekiller's mother used to beat little Johnny with a hatchet-handle. The act of murder was wrong. I believed that. Degrees of guilt? That was for somebody else to decide—a judge and jury. My job was to catch the murderer, and I intended to do it.

I looked up, surprised. They were back at the table. Maybe I'd been spending too much time alone lately. My mind was wandering a lot. Maybe it was Post-Traumatic Stress Syndrome; a fancy word for the shock of seeing your love with her face blown away.

I waited until I saw his head begin to bob, and I reached the table just as he was going under. I grabbed the back of his shirt and let him slump forward. She had been trying to figure out what was suddenly wrong with her date and hadn't seen me coming. She looked up, startled, and said, "What are you doing here?" Then she looked at the guy with his head on the table and back at me. She was very quick. "You did this?"

I nodded and sat down on the other side of the date, taking advantage of her surprise. "He'll just sleep for a while. Sorry, but I have to talk to you alone. I didn't kill your sister. I loved her and she loved me. Maybe we'd even have married some day, I don't know. All I know is she's gone and I'm trying to find out who murdered her. I think you can help. I don't know what your relationship with Grossman is, but I think he was involved in some way. I need your help to find the man who really murdered your sister."

I finished my speech and waited for the storm. It never came. Instead she just smiled.

"I'm sorry," she said. "I hope I didn't hurt you too bad. I was afraid Bobby would kill you. I don't believe you murdered my sister. I only pretended to believe it for Grossman's sake. I want to find out who murdered my sister at least as much as you do, and I agree with you—I think he was involved or knows something. But if I'm going to find out, it's important that he trusts me. Do you understand?"

Life is funny. All of my elaborate plans and here I was sitting there in shock with my mouth wide open. I just nodded my head and mumbled, "I think so."

"Okay Mr. Sage, help me get my date out of here and into a cab. There is usually one parked out front. What did you do, slip something in his drink while we were dancing?" I nodded again. "I should thank you. He was a good dancer, but otherwise a real bore. His father is on board the *Southern Cross* and I was supposed to entertain him while they talk business."

Between the two of us we managed to get him into a taxi, laying him in the driver's side of the back seat. Then we went around, got in the other side, and propped him up. He took up a lot of room so Gretchen and I were pressed together, and I grew warm from the feel of her. I was even a little dizzy, partly from the rapid turn of events, I suppose.

She gave the cabbie the directions and he started off. I was still speechless at finding Antiay's twin so warm and friendly toward me. I even imagined that she was getting excited by the press of our bodies against each other. She had stopped talking and we rode in silence. I knew I should be questioning her, but except for an acute awareness of her presence, my mind was blank.

I tried to think of something other than her body, and it was like we were on the same wavelength because she tried to push her date over, bracing herself with her right hand on the back of the front seat. It was then I noticed the narrow zig-zag band of silver she was wearing on her wrist. For a moment I couldn't speak, but I took a deep breath and said, "You're wearing Antiay's bracelet."

She was leaning forward and she looked back at me nervously. "I got it from her...things."

"I gave it to her," I mumbled. Something was starting to click in my mind, like in a movie theater when the film slips on the sprocket.

"Do you want it back?" It was almost a whisper. A ghost of a whisper.

My mind continued to click on the broken sprocket. On the screen was Antiay's body sprawled on the bed...something I had been trying to remember...her arm dangling from the bed...the bracelet...her arm...the bracelet...her arm—her arm! Something exploded in my mind. Her left arm! The bracelet was on the left arm of the corpse. Antiay always wore it on her right arm—she never took it off. That meant—I leaned back and everything fell into place. That meant this was—

"Antiay?" I said, tears streaming down my cheeks.

She turned toward me, tears flooding from her own eyes. "Yes," she whispered, laying her head against me. "Yes, yes, I'm sorry Rick...yes, it's me."

Chapter Twelve

LOVE, ANGER, AND relief: a kaleidoscope of emotions washed over
me. Even a moment of doubt—was this some new trick? Gretchen
pretending to be Antiay? But in my heart I knew it wasn't. This was her,
really her, and I held her close—to feel the reality of it. She cried quietly
and hugged me back saying again and again, "I'm sorry, I had to do it, I'm
sorry..."

I brushed my hand against her cheek as if that would stop the flood
of tears. "It doesn't matter, Antiay, I understand. You were right, I
wouldn't have let you do it—I couldn't have. It's all right, I understand."

She raised her face to mine and we kissed. The doubt, anger, and
loneliness evaporated. Only love remained, and the salt-sweet taste of
tears and lips too long apart. It was a long kiss running hot, and I think we
would have shed our clothes right there, oblivious to our surroundings, but
the taxi stopped in front of the gates of a walled estate.

It was like we were tumbling in free-fall and it took seconds before
we could respond to the cabby's cynical grin. We looked at each other and
laughed, a little hysterically I suppose. We were shocked to find ourselves
there in that taxi, with Gretchen's unconscious date sharing the back seat,
snoring.

We got out and I carried the unconscious man over my shoulder to
the door of the house. After a moment, a servant opened the door and
Antiay explained that our friend had drunk too much at a party. The
servant led us inside, I deposited him on a sofa, and we left.

Back in the taxi, we instructed the driver to return us to the
nightclub. Alone in the dark of the back seat we kissed again, but the spell
had been broken and this time we couldn't ignore for long our
surroundings, or the questions and explanations of the missing days which
crowded, unwanted, into our minds.

"Are you all right?" Antiay asked, feeling gently the battlescars on
my face.

"Yeah, I'm better than all right, now. As long as you don't leave me
again. Do we have time? Will you be missed if you don't return to the
Southern Cross?" Implicit in my tone was my determination that no way
would I let her out of my sight now.

"No, luckily the arrangements were that I would rent a car and meet the *Southern Cross* back in La Paz. I was to entertain the son while Jurgen worked on the father. He gave me plenty of time. Later tonight, after the father returns to shore, another man, a Colombian, is to go on board, then they're returning to La Paz."

"You weren't going to spend the night with that guy?"

She laughed and touched my lips with her finger. I guess I'd shouted. Then she opened her purse and took out something she held up for me to see in the passing lights. It was a foil packet like the one I'd used to knock out her date. "Remember when you gave me this?" she said. "You told me it might come in handy sometime. It's lucky we didn't both put them in the same drink. I was about ready. I really wanted some time to myself and I was looking forward to being off the *Southern Cross* for a day."

I laughed. "It's a good story anyway. I'm just glad we have some time to sort things out. I'd have hated to start out our new life with a fight."

"Yes, lucky for us." She kissed my cheek. "Where shall we go? We should get away from the Cape, just in case."

"The Hotel California? I've waited this long, I guess one more hour won't be too hard."

She smiled at me—that smile. "I'm sure you're wrong about that. And the Hotel Californicate sounds perfect."

It was an old joke of ours. We'd stayed there before. "Yeah, you're right, it's going to be a hard ride." We kissed again and my hand found her warm inner thighs, but once more the taxi stopped and the driver flashed his grin.

"*Más tiempo?*" he asked. "*Un paseo cerca el oceano?*"

"*No gracias,*" I replied, "*Bailar es amar.*"

He shrugged, and I paid him.

We retrieved the Hog and I got out my leather jacket for Antiay. She gave me a look when she saw the cannon. I ignored it, and soon we were on the highway. What was left of the waning moon laid a moonbeam across the ocean, and with Antiay pressing into my back, her arms wrapped around me and her hands warming in my crotch, I was as close to heaven as St. Peter at the gates.

An hour later, we were banging on the door of the Hotel. Alfredo opened after we nearly woke the dead. He shook his head when he recognized us, and pretended to be grumpy. "Ah, you have the fever again I see," he said. "I have told you, you should not ride that motorcycle in the night. The hot and cold together, it is bad for you. And it is bad for me also if I do not sleep."

We laughed and offered our apologies.

"You are lucky," he said as he went behind the desk. "It is vacant." He tossed me the key to our favorite room.

"*Gracias* Alfredo. *Qué tenga un buen noche.*"

"It is unlikely," he said as we started up the stairs. "There will be much noise from above."

"That is true," I replied.

At the door to our room we stopped and I took her in my arms. On the ride from Cabo San Lucas my mind had been in turmoil. So many questions had come up in the last few days about Antiay's past, and they swirled amongst a flood of other questions about the death of her sister. But my curiosity was contained for the moment by relief and passion.

"We have a lot to talk about," I said.

"Yes. We do. But I'm not in much of a talking mood." Her hand moved down from my back and pulled me closer to her.

"Me, either. What do you say we leave all that for over breakfast?"

She kissed my lips, wrapped a leg around mine and murmured, "*Mmmmhmm.*"

I fumbled with the key, but finally the door swung open and we stumbled inside, awkward as two blindfolded kids in a three-legged race.

IN THE MORNING, our usual table with fresh fruit and chilled champagne was set up on the balcony overlooking *Todos Santos*. For a few moments we watched in silence, nibbling pineapple slices and grapes, as school children passed by the candy maker sweeping the walk in front of his shop. Somewhere nearby a Mockingbird ran through his repertoire.

One of us had to bring it up. Might as well be me. "Antiay, I'm sorry, but we have to talk about this...why you didn't let me know you were still alive. It's true I wouldn't have let you do what you did. That was very dangerous." I took a sip of champagne, giving her time to respond, but she sat there, staring off into space.

"So when you found her body like that, you believed the murderer thought he had killed you. You figured you could find the killer if he thought you were really dead. You left your things there, including the bracelet I'd given you. You counted on that to convince me—to keep me from looking too close. Except that her right arm was under the body and covered with blood, so you put it on the left arm, counting on—"

"I didn't really think it all out so coldly as it sounds when you say it, Rick," she blurted out, a single tear running down her cheek. She wiped at it, covering her face with her hands. I knew she was involuntarily replaying that looped memory of her sister, lying there on that bed....

"I know, I know, Antiay...I didn't mean to make it sound like that.

It's the detective in me. You learn to do that—to compartmentalize your emotions. I'm sorry. I know almost exactly how you felt. I thought it was you, remember? But we have to talk about this. We have to get past it somehow, and then we'll find the bastard who did it, together."

"Yes, okay, I know. It's all right," she said, looking up at me with tears streaming down her face. I reached over and took her hand. She squeezed it and wiped at the tears. "I've gone over and over it. At first I'd get hysterical and break down crying, but then it became like you said. I had to think about it logically, without emotion overwhelming me, so I've separated it all somehow, mostly. I've built a kind of dam. In some ways it was cold, what I did there in that room after the initial shock. Something came over me—hate and anger I guess, and I reacted almost without thinking."

"What made you think someone had meant to kill you instead of Gretchen?"

"I don't know. Intuition I guess. It was my apartment and I was the only one who knew she was coming. I believe she surprised someone and they thought it was me. Otherwise, it was too much coincidence. I guess I got that from you. I couldn't believe it was all some kind of horrible accident. Besides, guns are very tightly controlled in Mexico."

"Yes, and the fact you're still alive now seems to prove the killer thought it was you. Otherwise he would have known you'd taken her place. That was quite a gamble."

"Yes, I suppose." Her tears had stopped flowing. She wiped away the last of them and took my hand again. "Anyway, the rest was as you described it. I made it seem like it was me. I traded purses...and put my bracelet on her, like you said. And I took some things the killer had left there—"

"What were they? Do you still have—"

"Easy, Mr. Detective. Evidently someone wanted to set me up. To make it look like...anyway, there was some cocaine, and...some pictures..."

"I've seen a copy of one of them Antiay. The governor showed me. It was his son with...with her. They tried to blackmail the governor and—"

"Over the gambling?"

"Yes."

"I see. That's the bad side of being an identical twin. They can blame everything on both of you. Or either one. And you thought...?"

"I didn't know about your sister then. I thought...I couldn't believe it, but..."

"It's all right, it's my fault. I never told you anything. About my sister...anything. Because you were different, it was a different life—I didn't want to mix it all up yet. My past...I just wanted a new start. But then one day, there it was—the past anchored right out there in La Paz Bay. I should have known..."

"Antiay, maybe you should start at the beginning."

"Yes, I guess so, wherever that is. I'm not really sure now. I suppose, it's when our parents were taken away...we were from East Berlin. They were arrested as traitors. It was horrible. Maybe they were traitors—at least, now I hope so. But you can realize...at the time? Anyway, Uncle Jurgen—"

"Uncle Jurgen?"

"Yes, Jurgen Grossman is my mother's brother."

"Jesus!"

"So you begin to see. He was very influential with the government. Now I know he was with the Secret Police, the Stasi, but at that time we were little girls."

Antiay got that faraway look again and stopped talking. I waited, and after a couple of minutes she continued.

"Uncle Jurgen had us brought into his office and we stood there in front of his desk. I'll never forget it. We were very scared. You can imagine. He told us he could save our parents—that there was no doubt of their guilt, and even his position with the government was in danger. But he said he could keep them from being executed. He would do it for us, even though they were traitors, but we could never expect to see them again. He said the government would allow him to raise us, but it would be difficult because he was single. He never has married. Anyway, we were to do everything he asked of us. If we caused problems, our parents might be shot."

"What a bastard."

"Yes, I guess I hated him even then, but Gretchen was afraid. I was always the stronger one. She would always say, you are the strong one, I'm the pretty one. It was an old joke between us. So I always tried to cooperate because Gretchen would beg me not to cause problems. Still, there were a few times...but mostly I tried to look out for Gretchen. I guess I failed in the end though."

"It wasn't your fault."

"The murder? I don't know—maybe not. I wasn't talking about that though. But it's better if I continue with this story—you will see what I mean.

"Gretchen and I were trained as Stasi agents—"

"But you were just kids."

"Kids make excellent spies, because no one suspects them. They impressed on us continually how lucky we were to be accepted even though we were the children of traitors. And we had to prove ourselves. To show we weren't there just because of our uncle. I suppose it's hard to understand, but we had become convinced by that time that somehow our parents had betrayed even us. Anyway, we worked hard to be accepted and excelled in our training. I was looking forward to growing up and receiving an assignment of my own. I guess I really just wanted to be free of Uncle Jurgen.

"Then came the end of communism in Russia, and the fall of the Berlin Wall. For a while, we made our way hiding out in different communist countries. Uncle Jurgen convinced us we would all be shot if we were caught. I was miserable and cried a lot. During this time, Gretchen was the strong one. She said it wasn't so bad. At least we were together. But she actually liked Uncle Jurgen. It's funny how we could be so alike and yet sometimes react to things so differently. My way was to rebel—to fight back. Hers was to try to please everyone. She wanted everyone to be happy. But I know that underneath she wasn't happy either. It was an act that became harder and harder to perform."

"I wish I had known her, Antiay."

"Yes, you would have liked her, in spite of...well, underneath she was a better person than me..."

Antiay stopped talking for a moment and I didn't interrupt her thoughts. She sipped her champagne. I poured her some more, then she went on.

"Anyway, we worked for Uncle Jurgen, and eventually, when he bought the *Southern Cross*, we all moved aboard. He had a lot of money in Swiss bank accounts, and after awhile, after the West lost interest in prosecuting ex-spies and started hiring them, he used his connections in the spy world to start freelancing for anyone who would pay.

"Sometimes no one knew we were related. It's part of the way we operated. It wasn't all distasteful of course. We cruised to exotic ports and at times it was exciting—even fun. For the last two years I was onboard, we were based in Mazatlán. But I always felt a bit like a prisoner, even at the best of times. We never had a life of our own, Gretchen and me. Our job was mainly to entertain and spy on the clients or whoever he wanted information on.

"Gretchen had a Mexican boyfriend in Mazatlan and she started doing a lot of cocaine. She'd already been drinking a lot and partying too much, so I tried to talk to her about it, but she'd either cry or get mad at me. I tried to get Uncle Jurgen to do something, too. He said I was worried about nothing. He said I should loosen up and have some fun myself. I realized then he was actually encouraging her destructive behavior. I know now I should have done something. That's what I meant by letting her down."

"Did you meet her boyfriend? Do you know his name?"

"No, I never met him. By then we weren't doing much together anymore. I didn't hang out with her crowd. I really wanted out by then, but I couldn't bring myself to split up with Gretchen. I mentioned it to her once, and she thought I was crazy.

"I don't know why, but for a long time I hadn't even thought about my parents. I didn't remember what they looked like and we didn't have any pictures, because they were traitors. I'd put them out of my mind years ago. Well, not put them out really, as it turned out, but just buried it all—sealed it up in some corner of my mind.

"It was the dream that did it. I had a dream about them and it was very vivid. I was a little girl—Gretchen wasn't in the dream for some reason—and I was going on a picnic in the park with my mom and dad. Their faces were kind of fuzzy, like in dreams sometimes, but somehow I knew they were my parents.

"It was a beautiful summer day and the grass was very green and there were flowers, like in a painting. We had a big basket on a blanket and we started to take the food out of the basket. There was an enormous amount of food—everything you could imagine, enough for a hundred people really. But we just kept taking it out, and then the dream changed. My mother said we couldn't possibly eat all of this food, then my dad said we can't eat this food, and my mother agreed that, no, we can't eat this food, and they started to change. They got older and older looking and they turned all to gray, their faces and everything, so that they looked like dead people, but they kept saying over and over that they couldn't eat the food. Then the police came and took them away, and I was sitting by the food crying and sobbing that it was all right, they could eat the food. And I woke up crying and thinking about my parents, for the first time in years.

"It was that morning I realized my parents might have been released from prison and maybe didn't know how to contact us. Suddenly I didn't care anymore whether they'd been traitors or not. I realized that I never really cared about any of that. I'd just pretended, burying it all.

"So I went to Jurgen and told him I wanted to quit, that I was going back to Germany to find my parents, and I was going to take Gretchen with me.

"He became very angry and called me a fool. He said I was ungrateful for all he'd done for us, and went on and on about why couldn't I be nice like my sister...she appreciated what he'd done, but I'd always been difficult.

"I told him I didn't care what he thought or said about me. I was going home to find my parents. He said if I went he would cut me off from any money. He had always controlled our money, handing it out like an allowance. I said I didn't care anymore what he did, I was leaving.

"Then he laughed—that weird little laugh of his that comes out when he quits pretending to be nice. When he stopped laughing, he grinned, and said my parents were already dead. They'd been shot right after they were arrested. Did I really think they'd keep them alive just for two little girls? Two little traitor girls?

"I told him we were leaving, immediately, and if he tried to stop us he should be careful because I knew a lot about his operations. He just laughed again and said I was free to go, but Gretchen wouldn't go anywhere—that she liked the good life and her cocaine too much. I said she would when she learned about our parents. He laughed even harder. 'She already knows', he said. 'She already knows.'

"Of course I confronted Gretchen about it and she told me it was true. Years ago she had been crying about our parents and asked him if she couldn't see them. He'd told her then, but made her promise not to tell me because I'd be too upset. She had agreed, and never told me.

"She said she was sorry, and I knew she had only been trying to protect me. But I was angry anyway. I told her I was leaving, but she could stay if she wanted to. That was a mistake. I should have begged her to go with me. She begged me to stay. She said she was in love and couldn't leave. I told her I had to leave—that I might do something I'd regret if I didn't get out of there. Anyway, we argued over it for a while, but finally I left. I just couldn't forgive her for not telling me about our parents. The *Southern Cross* was moored in Mazatlán then, not far from the Hydro ferry. A few hours later I was in La Paz. About six months after that I met you."

"Damn Antiay, I wish you'd told me. It sounds like you needed to talk to someone. You've been carrying a lot of guilt you don't deserve."

"Maybe Rick. But I don't even understand or believe it all myself. Now it seems like some fantastic sordid magazine story. 'I was a Teenage Spy,' or something. Anyway, I was going to tell you...at the right time. Guess I waited too long."

"No, sometimes we don't have the freedom to choose that we think we do. The choices appear so stark in hindsight and we forget the infinite possibilities that existed beforehand—including knocking the pieces off the board. I don't know if that makes any sense. What I'm trying to say is that Gretchen's death isn't the result of anything you did or didn't do. It's the result of someone's finger squeezing the trigger mechanism of a .44 caliber handgun. There were infinite possibilities up until that instant. Someone chose death, shot Gretchen, and became a murderer. Our responsibility is to find that killer. Nothing else can be done except to shed tears and bury the dead."

"I've done those things already, although I won't really be able to grieve for her until this is over. I suppose that's a decision I made when I saw her body. She was dead and the only thing I could do for her was to find her killer."

"Yeah, that's how I felt when I saw her and thought it was you. You know, you're lucky your Uncle didn't figure out you were pretending to be Gretchen. Maybe you looked alike, but it sounds like your personalities were really different. It didn't take me long to decide it was you."

"Yes, but that's because you couldn't believe someone could be just like me."

"That's true I guess. It was the bracelet that gave it away—and how I felt, being so close to you."

"The thing that helped me fool Uncle Jurgen was that he expected it to be Gretchen. Still, there was one time I almost gave it away. It was the bracelet then, too. See, even though there were differences in our personalities, physically we were very identical and we loved that. We were careful to dress alike and wear our hair the same way. It wasn't hard because we usually chose the same things anyway. But if we were mad at each other—which wasn't very often because we couldn't stand it for long—then we'd wear different things just to spite each other. As we got older it actually bothered us to wear anything different because it felt like we were having a fight."

Tears started to stream down Antiay's cheeks again, and she tried to wipe them away. I'd had the same problem with tears when I thought she'd been murdered, so I didn't interrupt her. I knew it had to run its course.

A couple of minutes later she had it under control. "I'm sorry. Where was I?"

"The bracelet."

"Yes. We were like two parts of the same person. I don't know how to explain it except maybe it's like a person with a split personality. That's why it was so easy to pretend to be her. A part of me is like her. We used to do imitations of our differences just to tease each other.

"Anyway, when we were babies they put bracelets on us, on opposite wrists, in order to tell us apart. Gretchen's was on her left and mine on my right. As we grew up we continued to do that. It worked two ways for us.

When we wanted to be recognized we could be, but if we wanted to change identities to trick someone we'd switch our bracelets to the other side. We even pulled a switch on boyfriends a few times, until we found out we didn't like the same type of guys.

"This probably all sounds strange, but looking alike was really important to us. After we lost our parents we only had each other. I remember we had a big fight about it once, because Gretchen hated wrist watches and I wanted one. It was one of our few differences like that. I thought she was just being stubborn so I got one anyway and started wearing it. She wouldn't give in though and for about a week we wore the opposite of everything. I don't know how many times we changed clothes just because the other had on something similar. Finally she got her way by threatening to have her hair cut really short—knowing I would hate that. So I got rid of the wristwatch and just carried it in my pocket or my purse. She could be difficult when she wanted to be. And I was supposed to be the stubborn one. I guess I'm getting off the track though."

"I don't care. I like hearing you talk about her. I wish I could have seen you together."

"Yes...I was looking forward to that. I was hoping we could make up when...but then I found her...damn..."

She started to cry again and I was holding back tears, too. "Maybe we shouldn't talk about it right now Antiay. We can do it later."

"No, I want to. It helps to talk. I've been keeping it all in. Like I was saying, it was easy to be Gretchen. After I got the bracelet and the other things back from that place, I started wearing it on my left wrist like Gretchen would have. Actually, wearing it helped me feel closer to you. But then I had it off polishing it and I was thinking about you and I must have just unconsciously put it back on my right arm. Uncle Jurgen noticed it right away.

"He looked at me with that raised eyebrow and that eagle-eye look he gets and he said, 'Gretchen, why are you wearing that bracelet the way Antiay would?' Maybe other differences had already been bothering him and the bracelet set it off. He's extremely intelligent—after all he's made a career out of deception. I thought it was all over, but like you said, I must be a good actress. And I knew all of her mannerisms.

"I said, 'I don't know, Uncle. I was missing Antiay so I wore it the way she would.' Then I looked sad the way Gretchen would have—the way she always did to get her way with him. 'If it bothers you I'll change it back.'

"He thought about it a moment like he was trying to figure out why it was bothering him. Then he said, 'Well it seems morbid, but if it makes you feel better go ahead.'"

"That was close."

"At the time I was sorta crazy. The worst thing, is I haven't found out much about who killed her. Have you figured anything out?"

I told her about the events of the past few days—that in many ways I felt like I'd just been banging my head against a brick wall. I meant it literally, and she laughed, covering her mouth and saying it must be the champagne. Then she started to cry too, and I laughed, saying her tears hurt me worse than her laughing at me.

Hell! We were both emotional and feeling a little wacky. Little wonder. Anyway, I told her that with the governor and the chief prosecutor on our side, we could make some waves if we had some evidence.

"But the only damn suspect I can come up with who'd want to harm you is, Grossman, and even that is a stretch."

"I still don't know either. I keep thinking...Uncle Jurgen let me go before. Why would he want to kill me now?"

"I don't know. It could be the killer didn't intend to kill you when he went to your apartment."

"Yes, that's possible. Maybe someone was going to frame me for drugs. And—"

"And Gretchen surprised them. Why was she at your apartment? Remember, you told me when you left that day, that you had to meet someone?"

"Yes, that was her."

"At first I thought you had gone to meet the killer. Why were you meeting Gretchen—I mean any particular reason?"

"I don't know really. The day before I'd found a note under my door saying she'd been there, but I wasn't home, and she'd return the next evening at six-thirty.

"I'd contacted her right after the *Southern Cross* appeared in the harbor. I guess I was a little cruel. I told her in a note that I didn't want to see her unless she was off cocaine and wanted to leave the *Southern Cross*. I just couldn't go through all of that again, even though I missed her terribly. She never responded. I found out when I took her place that she'd refused to go into La Paz. She never went to shore there, except to go out to the Mission Hotel on the Mogote. I think she stayed away for my sake. That's why I was surprised when I got her note. In it she said she had something very important to discuss with me—something that was going to make me very happy."

"It could be she was planning to leave the *Southern Cross*, and she told your uncle. Then he decided to set you up. While he was planting the stuff she walked in, and he thought it was you. Maybe he didn't think to lock the door behind himself...he was hurrying...then she walked in. I'm not convinced it was your uncle, but whoever the killer was, it could have happened that way. Would she have done that—just walked in?"

"Sure. I was a little late and she must have arrived a little early. We had been very close. We never knocked on each other's doors or anything. If she was in a happy mood and wanted to surprise me she would have tried the door and walked in. I know because I would have done the same. We were like that."

"Could it be Bobby? I mean would your Uncle have sent him to do it?"

"No. Definitely not. I was closer to Bobby than to Uncle Jurgen. Bobby was our protector—our guardian. I don't think he'd do anything to hurt either one of us."

"Even if your uncle ordered him?"

"No. I'm sure of it. He'd refuse. He was prepared to die for us. He actually cried when I left the boat—when I kissed him goodbye. Uncle Jurgen knows it, too. I don't even think he'd ask him. Maybe one of the other crew members, but not Bobby. Not for that."

"Okay. Since you've been back on the *Southern Cross*, as Gretchen, has your uncle left the boat for any long period of time—like overnight?"

"No."

"Have you been able to find out why Gretchen wanted to see you? Has your Uncle mentioned anything about her leaving?"

"No, but that's not unusual. You have to understand—it's his method with us. After an argument, he'd just pretend nothing had happened. He wouldn't bring it up and we'd be afraid to—especially Gretchen. If she really told him she wanted to leave, and he said no, then she'd have to do it secretly if she still intended to. He'd never give in. Even when he agreed to our requests, he'd only talk about it once. After that he'd say, 'Just do it—it's already been decided.' That's the way he is. So I still don't know for sure why she wanted to see me."

"Antiay, there's something else I haven't told you."

"What's that?"

"Your sister's boyfriend, the governor's son, the guy in the photograph with her—his name is Victor and he's been murdered, too."

"My God! Do you think the same person did it. The same one who—"

"I don't know. Nothing makes sense. If it was blackmail, over the gambling thing, why kill off Victor? It's too bad we don't know why

Gretchen wanted to see you—it might tell us a lot. It all seems connected, but there's a big piece to this puzzle that's missing. I can't figure out why—"

"Rick."

I was staring off, I guess, so the tone of her voice startled me. I looked at her and it was like she had transformed into a different person. A cold person consumed with hatred. A person I had seen before in a hundred different versions. Usually they were standing over fresh corpses. It scared me. Like the song says, there's fifty ways to lose your lover.

"I'm going to kill him, Rick. Whoever did this, I'm going to shoot their face off if I can—like he did to my sister. I want you to know that, and please, don't try to stop me or talk me out of it. I want him dead, and I'm going to be the one to do it."

I couldn't stand to see her like that so I looked away. There was nothing to say in the face of rage. In the past few days I had endured the same volcanic emotions. It was like a plague and the carrier was a murderer. If he died in the midst of the devastation he'd caused, who could say it wouldn't be justice? Antiay had lost her parents to executioners, and her twin sister to a killer. Should I whisper sweet clichés about law and justice in her ear?

I stood up and took her hand. Our morning had been ruined, as we had known it would. For this new Antiay, beauty would always be tinged with sadness when it brought memories of her sister.

She stood up, we hugged, then we went inside and laid together on the bed. Her rage softened to tears, and after a while came full circle back to love.

Later we talked some more about our plans. The mystery goes out of detective work when you learn that one thing just follows another, like life. All you really need to bring to it is persistence, and an unquenchable curiosity.

I told her my plans had more or less ended at Cabo San Lucas, and I'd have to formulate a new one. I asked about her plan, and she told me.

"I decided to use the same weapon they tried to use against me. I have a little camera we were issued by the Stasi and I took some pictures of my uncle with that guy from the DEA."

"Bill White?"

"Yes."

"Wow! Great."

"I also took some pictures of Uncle Jurgen with the guy from the cartel. I decided that at some point, I'd have to reveal myself to my uncle and force him to confess, or to tell me what he knows."

"That's dangerous."

"I don't care. Anyway, I wanted to try to record some of his conversations with these guys, but I didn't have enough warning to set it up."

"Hey, I have a great tape I made of White talking about Grossman If we put that together with the photographs, we'd really be holding a hammer over him. Where's the film? Have you developed it yet?"

"No. I have it with me in my purse."

"Great. We can get it developed at a one-hour place when we get back to La Paz."

"Okay. But I still don't know exactly how to go about using it. I was going to just keep pretending to be Gretchen, and hope I'd find out something more. I guess I really think it's my uncle's fault, whatever happened. But I wanted to be sure. I'm not convinced he'd tell me anything even if I told him I was sending pictures of him and a United States DEA agent to the Colombian cartels. He'd probably—"

"Kill you."

"I don't think so. Anyway, I was going to set it up so the information would get to the cartels even if he did get me first. That way I'm sure they would take care of him for me."

"Except, I don't intend to lose you again so we'll just have to come up with a better plan. But I agree with you that your uncle seems to be the key. With your pictures and my tape, maybe we can turn that key. By the way, who is the Colombian on board?"

"His name is Jorge Escudero. He's high up in one of the cocaine cartels. I think those crates you saw being loaded are weapons the cartel is buying. I don't know the details because they didn't discuss it in front of me, but I saw them being stored in the secret hold in the hull of the boat. The *Southern Cross* was built especially for this kind of thing. The secret hold is under the main engine. They actually have to lift the front of the engine up to get into it, and it's all set up so they can do it in about five minutes. Uncle Jurgen always complains about it though, because it means the *Southern Cross* is dead in the water when the hold is open."

"Sounds like quite a system. Do you know when the delivery is going to be made?"

"Not exactly, but Uncle Jurgen said to be aboard back in La Paz by eight o'clock this evening—that we have to make a run to Espíritu Santo, that big island a couple of hours north of La Paz.

"I said that was great, I could do some diving, but he said no, we'd only be anchored in Partida for a few hours and then we'd be coming back to La Paz. He said he wanted me along in case he needed someone to translate. Uncle Jurgen speaks excellent Spanish but he has a bad German accent. Sometimes they can't understand everything he says—so anytime he was worried about having a misunderstanding he would always use one of us. Gretchen and I both spoke fluently, without a German accent."

"Yeah, like your English I imagine. I don't know how you do it."

"A lot of practice, Rick. You should work harder on your Spanish."

"Yeah, I know. If we ever get this mess settled I intend to do just that. No more bowling for me until I learn my Spanish."

She laughed. It was another inside joke of ours.

"Oh, no," she said, "I don't want you to give up on our bowling."

"I guess that's too drastic. But back to business. It sounds like they're planning to make an exchange all right. I don't want you at risk any longer than necessary. What do you say we go for broke—can you sneak me aboard?"

"Sure, probably. After dark."

"Okay, I'll time it so I'm climbing aboard on one side of the boat when you're being welcomed on the other side. Is there a place to hide?"

"I guess you could get in the ski boat. It's on deck and has a cover. Then I could sneak some clothes to you and get you into my cabin once we're under way."

"Is there a way other than through the main salon?"

"Sure. There's an entrance from the cabins directly to the deck."

"Sounds great. We'll get extra copies of the pictures made and I'll make copies of the tape. Then I'll make arrangements with Hal Lewis to mail off a copy if anything happens to us. Who knows, maybe tonight we'll catch us a murderer."

"Let's drink to that," she said, jumping out of bed and grabbing a towel to wrap around herself as she went out on the terrace. She returned with the second unopened bottle of champagne, and two glasses. I popped the cork and she dropped her towel in pretended surprise. I quickly joined her, and standing stark naked in the middle of the room, we lifted two glasses of bubbly in a toast.

"To justice," I said, clinking her glass.

"To revenge," she replied, clinking mine. We drank then to our separate toasts, as I watched the cold determination return to her eyes, and realized a chasm of rage still separated our mutual goal.

Chapter Thirteen

WE WERE GETTING ready to leave for La Paz. I mean we got as far as the shower. But then a series of light touches grew to a snowball of wet kisses and climaxed in an avalanche tumbling onto the bed. Say it was one for good measure, or just for old time's sake, or to celebrate my uncle's seventy-first birthday on Thursday of next week. Any excuse for a party would do.

The ride to La Paz was like a dream. We were fairly satisfied in every way except sleep, but who wants to sleep when the waking world is so ripe. It was four o'clock when we left TodosSantos, and we dreamed our way in a warm wind until we arrived in La Paz at just after five.

I drove down *Jalisco* to the bus station where there were always plenty of cabs, and pulled over. We got off the bike, reluctantly, and Antiay looked up at me, waiting. Parting was going to be difficult.

"I guess we should split up here," I said. "The Hog attracts too much attention. Besides, we haven't got a lot of time. Do you want to take a taxi and get the pictures developed?"

"Sure. Three copies?"

"Sounds good. Then drop off the negatives and two copies at Hal Lewis' boat. I have to get him to take me out near the *Southern Cross*, so I'll go down to the marina after I make copies of the tape. Maybe we'll meet there."

"I can hardly stand to leave you, Rick. I'm really afraid. Not for myself—I mean afraid that we've had our last time together."

We hugged each other then, for a long moment.

"Antiay, we're going to finish this and then we're going to take a long ride on the mainland—maybe do the Copper Canyon train trip and ride the bike back. Nothing's going to stop us. Okay?"

"If you say so, big guy. See you later, huh?" She kissed me quickly and left, running across the road for a cab, waving goodbye but not looking back. She hadn't been able to hide the shine of tears in her eyes, and I had a reservoir of my own just behind a weak dam.

The cab pulled away and I watched it round a corner. She was gone, and the last few days had taught me it could be forever. I'd tried to sound confident, but murder had shattered our feelings of invulnerability. We both knew what we were going to do was very dangerous. It was a gamble—with our lives as high stakes. But I also knew we had to force the issue. The longer Antiay went on with her charade, the more dangerous it became for her. It was better to take the chance now while surprise was on our side. If the governor made his decision in Grossman's favor, the opportunity would fade away—along with most of the players. Front men would take over, and we'd be fighting an army of shadows. Tomorrow was the last day before the recipient of the casino license would be announced.

The world was a dangerous place, and I hadn't wished it to be otherwise until now. It was why I'd avoided emotional entanglements for so many years. Even with Antiay, we both tried to play by those rules, for our own separate reasons. And failed, ironically, because of murder.

I walked into the bus station to make my phone calls. For insurance. I knew Antiay intended to kill Grossman herself if she found out he was involved in the murder of her sister. She had enough other reasons to hate him, that I couldn't be sure she wouldn't try to do it anyway. I wouldn't allow that to happen, so if none of this worked, I might be forced to do the job for her. I didn't want to, but in this case, road-kill would be a worse crime. Besides, I knew he wasn't going to go meekly, without a fight. We'd be very lucky to get out of this in one piece ourselves. The odds were very stacked against us, which was appropriate considering there were Las Vegas connections.

I dropped a nickel into a pay phone slot. In this case a nickel was a peso coin, but a nickel would always be a nickel, by any other name. I dialed the number and the governor's assistant answered. I didn't trust him, even if the governor did, but I had no choice so I said "Mogote," and told him what I wanted and why. He said he didn't know if it could be done. He'd pass it on to the governor, but it would take a few hours before he had an answer. I told him I'd be out of touch so they'd just have to go ahead if they could. For emphasis I said, "Tell the governor this is our best chance, maybe our only chance to stop them. I've done all I can and now it's up to him. If he can't do it, well, who knows, maybe Baja Sur would make a great fifty-first state after all."

I hung up. A few minutes later I pulled into my place and perked up the guy in the white Ford who had it staked out. They knew I was on the loose again. I thought they would.

I figured there would be lots of guns on board the *Southern Cross,* and if I wasn't slowing down I should be able to get one of theirs if I needed it. So I put the cannon back in its hiding place and made some fresh coffee. I popped open a beer while I waited, and put the tape on, to copy. Then I took a shower and shaved again. I wondered why Grossman would risk everything by doing this weapons delivery now? At first it seemed like pure ego, but then I realized I was wrong. He'd never feel safer. The DEA evidently knew about it and they'd run interference, if necessary, with the *federales*. He thought he was covered, but he hadn't counted on the power of the concerned citizen.

I finished the tapes and put one in a manila envelope, which I addressed to Fred Metcalf with a note asking him to forward it to the Cali Cartel in Columbia. I knew, with his connections, he'd be able to find a way to get it to them. I just told him it would finally put a very gross man out of business. I put the original tape in with the cannon, drank my coffee, then slipped out the back and over the wall.

I'd decided to leave the Hog behind this time so the guy out front would have something to watch. I walked over to the *La Posada* and grabbed a cab. I gave the cabby directions to Freddy's office and when we arrived I had him wait for me. I climbed the stairs and walked into the reception area. The receptionist wasn't at her desk but the lights were on and the door to Freddy's office was open. I called out to him as I walked in.

"Freddy, you here?" He was there all right, with the receptionist on his lap.

"Hey, you busted me, *amigo*. We're doing overtime here." He laughed as the young woman scrambled off his lap trying to straighten what there was of a very short skirt. She disappeared into the outer office and I sat down.

"Guess I interrupted some undercover work. You know you can get in a lot of trouble in the U.S. for that sort of thing now. They call it sexual harassment."

"You can get in trouble here, too—if that had been her husband walking through the door."

"You should be more careful."

"Yes of course, but then life, it would be very dull. How was your date? Do I know her?"

"I hope not," I said smiling. I'd decided not to tell him about Antiay yet. It wasn't a matter of trust—more a question of who needed to know. I couldn't predict what was going to happen so it seemed safer not to tell anyone about Antiay's identity switch with her dead twin. There'd be time for that later. And besides, the less Freddy knew, the better off he was, in this case.

"Yes, maybe it is better you don't tell me her name, Rick. I have done much training of many women in this town."

"It's not what you have done that I'm worried about Freddy. It's what you might do."

"Yes, that, too, I'm afraid." He got up and walked over to the bar. "Scotch?" Freddy liked everything first class—women, clothes, cars and booze. In that order.

"Yeah, thanks. I'll have a quick one. I've only got a couple of minutes."

He handed me three fingers of single malt on ice, and asked, "What have you found out?"

"I don't want to go into it right now, Freddy. I'll fill you in later, if that's okay? You said you didn't want to get too involved."

"Sure, no problem. So you are still wrestling with the devil? I hope you don't get burned. Please be careful, my friend."

"Like you said, being careful makes for a very dull life. What did you find out about the guy from the Mafia?"

"*Nada*, I'm afraid. There don't seem to be any *gringos* in town who can't be accounted for. I think I can assure you there is no such person here. I have very good connections with the hotels, immigration, and others."

"Yeah, I know. Thanks. Is it possible they might have hired someone local?"

"*Sí*, it is possible. They have many contacts from the drug traffic. But there is no way to discover that information."

"Which makes for a good reason to do it that way. Freddy, I'd like you to check out everything you can on another person."

"I'll do what is possible. Who is this person?"

"The governor's assistant. Rafael Flores."

"*¡Ay!* You *are* wrestling with the devil. What kind of information do you require?"

"I don't know, anything unusual. Connections to the cocaine trade. Anything. Something. It's a fishing expedition."

"Okay Rick. I can locate the fish. But you would need some heavy equipment to bring him in."

"We'll worry about it when we get a strike." I downed the rest of the scotch, stood up and put the glass on the bar. "*Gracias*," I said as I turned for the door.

"*De nada*," he replied. "Good fishing."

The receptionist pretended to be busy as I hurried through, went down the stairs, and got into the waiting taxi. "*Marina de La Paz, por favor*," I said to the driver.

It was only a few minutes later when I got out of the cab and looked at my watch. Seven o'clock exactly. I paid the driver and headed for the docks. Poor old Steve was seated in his usual spot on his little wooden stool by the gates of the Marina. He had a battered coffee can at his feet and he was whistling some tune. Sailing off into the sunset didn't always lead to happily ever after. His wife got small boat fever and while they were anchored in La Paz, she jumped ship, sailing out of the harbor on a big yacht with some rich guy she met on the docks. Well, maybe she was happy. Steve whistled or played his guitar for change until he got enough together to drink himself to sleep. Some people gave him their heavy change every day. Others complained that he'd just drink it up. I didn't care. It was too late, you could see, for him to start over with new dreams. The ones in a bottle were all he could afford. His spirit had been busted.

I put some money in his can and asked him, "Did you see a beautiful blonde get out of a taxi and go in the Marina?"

"Come and gone," he replied. "Come and gone. They all come and go," he went on. "She's come and gone for sure."

I said, "Thanks Steve, have one on me," and walked on down to Hal's boat. I'd been sure Antiay wouldn't be there, for the same reason I'd stalled around. Too many good-byes in one day were hard on a person.

"*Hola.* Anybody home?" I knocked on the hull as I hollered, and in a second Hal's handsome, paint-smeared face popped out of the main hatch.

"Hey Rick, I was just thinking of you. I've been accused of being a psycho, but maybe they had it wrong. I'm just psychic."

"I don't think there's a category big enough to contain you Hal. Artist comes closest."

"I'm just glad my daddy didn't make no detectives."

"You're right about that."

"Come on aboard."

"Thanks." I followed him through the hatch into the main salon. I wasn't ready for the nude who welcomed me with open legs. "Jeez Hal, excuse me, I didn't know you had company." I was blushing and I'm not a very modest guy.

"Hey Rick, it's just a painting. What a schoolboy."

"Yeah, well, we haven't even been introduced."

"Okay. Amber, this is Rick Sage. Rick may I present Amber."

I made a bow. "Gee Amber, I feel like I know you already. Hal can't you get her a towel or something?"

"All right, all right. If you're gonna get all giggly about it, I'll put her up forward. I was just putting on some finishing touches. Do you like that pink?"

"Yeah sure, reminds me of someone I knew once." Amber was right out of Penthouse magazine. I know because I bought one once—to read an article about detectives in New York.

The painting Hal called Amber, was about the most explicit painting I'd ever seen. The subject was leaning back against what could have been Hal's mast. She had her arms behind her and around the mast like she might have been tied to it, although you couldn't see any rope. Whether she was tied or not, the expression on her face was definitely not protesting. But the thing about the painting was that she was seated just about eye-level—with her knees upraised and spread apart—so that the point of perspective arrived at a place a little below the reddish brown pubic patch where the pink from Hal's wet brush had just touched up the...well...it was something all right. "Hal, you know you could be arrested for this thing?" I said because I didn't know what else to say.

"Maybe. But you can be arrested for a lot of fun things, like what I did with the real Amber before and after I painted her. And a couple of times in between. I think I really captured her—she was something, Rick. Remember that woman I was going to meet the last time I saw you? That's why I was thinking of you just before you got here."

"Thank heavens that's the reason you were thinking of me."

"That and the fact that Antiay was here about twenty minutes ago. Hey, it's great she's still alive. Too bad about her sister though. She said you'd fill me in, but I'm not sure I want to know anything about it. Hey, anyway, Antiay really liked the painting. She said it was honest—at least from a man's point of view. I asked her if she'd pose for me some—"

I lunged for him but he ducked and my hand went right onto his palette of pinks. "Hal, you sonofabitch," I groaned. "Absolutely not, no way, or kiss your balls goodbye."

"Huh," he said, throwing me a towel, "That's sort of what she said only not quite so emphatically."

We both laughed. "How about some coffee? Or a beer?"

"Coffee would be great. I didn't get much sleep last night, and I'm scheduled for more of the same."

"Last night didn't have anything to do with Antiay did it? She looked great, but she also looked a little worried. Kind of how you look. It's wonderful that she's still alive—seems you guys should be happier."

"It was her twin sister who was murdered—by mistake. Antiay took her place on that yacht, the *Southern Cross*, hoping she could find out who the murderer is."

"See. She's been hanging around with the wrong guy. Better she should get her picture painted."

"Maybe you're right Hal. But I don't think I had anything to do with it. She's independent. She was close to her sister and she feels responsible in some way. Whoever killed her twin may have thought it was Antiay."

"Wow, the things going on in the world. I look out at night and all I see are stars above a peaceful harbor. And you didn't even know she had a twin sister?"

"It's a long story, but no, I didn't. For the last few days I've been looking for Antiay's murderer. Now I'm looking for the person who killed her sister, and I'm trying to keep Antiay alive. She won't listen to me so the best I can do is stay close. Did she leave some photographs?"

"I guess that's what this is."

He handed me an envelope and I took out the pictures. They were perfect—from several angles. White and Grossman together. I took a copy of each and put them in the envelope I'd brought the copy of the tape in. I sealed it and handed it to Hal. "I've got a couple of favors to ask you," I said.

"I hate to encourage you in this cloak and dagger stuff, but if you say it's got to be done, then I guess I'm with you."

"I appreciate your help, but if you have any doubts about it, I can find another way."

"No, it's not that. I could probably use a little adventure. The only problem is, I like you two a lot and I don't want anything to happen to you."

"With your help we'll have a much better chance of succeeding."

"Then it's settled. What do you want me to do?"

I told him about the envelope and asked him to mail it for me if I didn't come back. It was too bad he knew about Antiay. I wished she hadn't told him, and I hoped he was the only one, but we needed his help and maybe it wasn't fair not to tell him what he was getting into. I hadn't told Freddy all of the details because he was a professional and knew the rules. Besides, this kind of thing helped keep him in fancy clothes. But Hal was an innocent bystander we were involving in a dangerous business, however small his part. Anyway, it was done now.

So I told him about the *Southern Cross* and Antiay's connection with it. And about the smuggled weapons we suspected they were going to transfer to a fishing boat at the anchorage in Partida tonight. Then I told him what I wanted him to do. "Just take me in your dinghy and drop me off near the *Southern Cross* at eight o'clock. I'm going to sneak aboard while Antiay is being taken aboard the other side. Hopefully there'll be enough distraction with her arrival to cover me."

"Okay, but don't you think it would be better to do it with the Harbor Hog? We can raise the sails and it'll look like we're out for an evening cruise. Which I intend to do since we're going out anyway."

"Sounds great. They might take notice of a dinghy going close by, but they won't think anything of someone sailing past inside a busy harbor."

"Let's get with it then. I needed a good excuse to go sailing."

A few minutes late, we were motoring away from the dock, and once clear, we raised the sails and killed the engine. There was a light breeze blowing—just enough to send the Harbor Hog along at a good clip. It was a little before eight so we sailed around the harbor and cruised past the *Southern Cross* to check out the possibilities for getting aboard.

The tide was coming in, so that put their boarding ladder on the starboard side, facing La Paz. The port side was to the Mogote, and luckily the anchor chain was running out the port side of the bow. We couldn't see anyone on deck near the bow, but I figured any deck hands would be aft to bring aboard the launch and stow the gangplank after Antiay was aboard.

"Hal, do you think you can sail close enough so I can jump up to the anchor chain without going into the water? The lower part of that chain is liable to be slippery as a greased pole. If I can stay dry it should be easier."

"Sure. With this light breeze I can get so close you wouldn't want your fingers between us. I'll go slow and luff up, but we'll still be moving at a pretty good rate so it'll be a bit like a circus trapeze act."

"No problem. You get me close and I'll do the rest. It's eight o'clock and I can see the launch at the pier so it should be any minute now."

"Hey, we're in good position. I hope this works."

"Me, too." We tacked around for five more minutes until finally I could see Antiay, through Hal's binoculars. She climbed into the launch, and they pulled away from the pier heading for the *Southern Cross*. Antiay had made sure to give us plenty of time for error.

We tacked toward the *Southern Cross* at an angle to the bow as the launch neared the yacht and disappeared from our view. I climbed out on the starboard hull of the tri-maran, near the stern, and got ready for my leap.

I looked back and Hal gave me a thumbs-up as we raced closer. I thought we were going to miss by a mile for a moment, but Hal had the wind and the tide figured just right, and we slid within an inch of the chain as I took a deep breath and made the jump.

I reached the chain with momentum to spare, but my grip slipped and I started to slide down toward the water. Wrapping my legs tight around the chain, I pressed my fingers into the holes in the links, ripping the fingers of my left hand as they slid down one more link before I stopped. I was hanging there like an opossum, still a couple of feet above the water. I congratulated myself. Not even a wet foot. Hal had come around, tacking back along the starboard side of the yacht, and as I began my climb I heard a wolf whistle and Hal's voice shout, "Hey baby, how'd you like to go for a midnight cruise?"

Someone in a gruff voice hollered back, "You come that close to us again buddy and that hulk is gonna be a submarine."

Good for Hal. He got their attention that's for sure. I reached the top of the chain and swung a leg and then an arm over the rail. Then I was on deck making my way down the port side. A minute later I was under the cover of the ski boat, curled up for a nap.

It seemed only a few minutes, but it was more like an hour later that I felt a hand grab my leg. "Rick, it's me Antiay. Are you sleeping in there?"

"I was," I whispered, and grabbed her arm.

"Stop fooling around," she whispered back. "Come on."

I climbed out of the ski boat, joining her on deck. "Where are we?" I asked.

"We're just passing Pichilingue. C'mon. They're having a discussion in the salon and I was dismissed for a while."

We made our way to her quarters without being discovered. Once inside she turned on the lights, locked the door, and then wrapped her arms around my neck. "Whew," she whispered. "I'm glad that's over. Did you have any trouble getting aboard? When Hal sailed past and whistled at me, I was sure you made it."

"It was easy. But what's this I hear about you posing for Hal?"

"We're maybe about to die and you're worrying about something like that? Besides he said he'd pay me twenty dollars and it looked like fun."

"That figures. He said he paid Amber fifty."

"All right, all right. Truce! Before you make me cry. You know I wouldn't let him paint me nude...again."

I picked her up, carried her to the bed, and pinned her down on it as she whispered through her giggles, "I was just kidding. Stop before you make me start laughing out loud. *Shhh!* Someone might hear us."

I released her hands and kissed her. She was worse than me, laughing in the face of danger. She turned me on more than ever. I pressed forward, but she stopped me with a finger to my lips.

"There's something I have to tell you, Rick. There's an extra man on board. An American. He seems to be involved in the deal somehow."

"Is he with the guy from Columbia?"

"No, I don't think so. Uncle Jurgen is treating him kind of like a protégé. From what I could tell, the guy from the U.S. is buying from the cartel."

"Damn. I'll bet he's DEA"

"Why DEA? Uncle Jurgen wouldn't bring them on a weapons drop."

"Yeah, that's just it—what if it's a three-way deal? It makes sense. The DEA agent pretending to be a buyer, and your Uncle is the middleman. The cartel gets the weapons, the agent gets cocaine, and Uncle Jurgen Grossman gets the cash. That's why a VIP from the Cartel is here. I'll bet the agent is going to take over the business from your uncle, and then the DEA will have its own pipeline."

"But why would my uncle do that? It doesn't make sense. If the cartel finds out, he's a dead man. To actually introduce them to an agent of the DEA—it's suicide. Uncle Jurgen isn't stupid."

"Maybe he didn't have a choice. What if, say, the United States, Germany, and the Soviet Union decided they want to shut him down? So they threaten to prosecute him in Germany unless he cooperates with the DEA. White allows him to do a few more deals and they even help him to set up that partnership with the Mafia, bidding on the casino license. And they guarantee him immunity from prosecution. Maybe they even agreed to help him change identities. That's standard operating procedure for the CIA, FBI, DEA and the rest of the alphabet soup boys. It comes down to a question of who he would rather have mad at him—the major western governments, or the cartels."

"Uncle Jurgen retiring? But then, why would he have wanted to kill me?"

"I don't know. Maybe he got nervous. You were the one element not under his control. And here you were, living in La Paz. Maybe he didn't intend to kill you. It's possible he just wanted to scare you. Maybe blackmail. Who knows?"

"Those pictures! Could he really have had them taken? Damn the bastard!"

"Antiay, remember this is all just speculation. We might be wrong about part of it."

"But it makes sense. Would your DEA really—"

"It's not my DEA!"

"Okay, the DEA. Would they really help sell weapons in return for drugs?"

"Bill White would. It's no wonder he's in La Paz. This is his type of operation, setting up in the drug business. Maybe some innocent people get killed. White's excuse is they're getting closer and closer to the big guys, but somehow they never quite get them. Even if they do, some other smart hustler pops up to run things, and it just goes on and on with the lines between the so-called good guys and the bad guys becoming more and more blurred. They call it a war because to them that's an excuse to use any means."

Antiay pressed her finger to my lips. "*Shhh*, Rick...easy."

"Was I getting carried away?"

"A little."

"Sorry. Your sister is the second person I've known to lose their life in one of White's sleazy operations. Ah, never mind. I'm here with you and we've got a few hours until the showdown. That DEA guy complicates things, but we'll just have to muddle through. Do you have to go right back out there?"

"No, I said I had a headache and I was going to lie down. What do we do now?"

"I've been thinking a lot about shades of pink."

"Rick!"

"What?"

"*Mmmmm*. I forgot what I was going to say."

"You said, '*Mmmmm*.'"

"*Mmmmm-hmmmm...*"

Chapter Fourteen

IT WAS LIKE the evolution of the human race all over again. A long period of grunts and moans, and later we talked.

"I'm so sleepy, Rick. Do you think we have time for a nap?"

"Sure. It'll be at least a couple of hours before we get to the anchorage. If they want you they'll knock on the door, and I'll hide in the shower."

"Good. I don't feel like waiting around out there. Being with you again has taken some of the edge off my anger. I'm afraid I don't have it in me to pretend I'm Gretchen much longer. You know, we haven't talked much about what we're going to do. I mean, how we're going to go about it."

"I guess that's because we don't know what we're going to do. I was hoping you had a plan."

"Rick! Get serious."

"Yeah, okay. I was kidding. But really, we're going to have to improvise. I think we'll wait until they're busy with the transfer of the weapons. Then you get your uncle down here on some kind of pretext and we'll drop it on him—the photographs, the tape, and the fact Gretchen is dead and you're alive. When you first get him in here though, pull that little gun on him. I'll be hiding in the head and—"

"Rick! How did you—"

"Don't worry, I know. Just point it at him and ask about Victor. Tell him you know he killed him. Okay?"

"I think I can manage that all right."

"Then we're set. C'mere, let's take a nap." We curled up together and she was soon asleep. It took me awhile longer. I was worried about not letting her in on my real plan. But then I also knew she wasn't letting me in on hers. Antiay was intent on revenge and I'd just have to be ready for that. I knew how she felt but I was a detective, not a gunfighter. Unless I had no choice.

I got out of bed, did what I had to do, and slipped back in. I guess I finally drifted off to sleep, and when I woke up, Antiay was gone. I got out of bed in the dark, groped my way into the bathroom and splashed water on my face. I didn't really feel much better for the sleep, but I probably wasn't going to until this was over. It went with the territory, but the territory had been much easier to cover at twenty-five than it was now, as much as I hated to admit it.

I looked out of the porthole. An ocean-going tuna boat was tied up next to us. The deck lights were off, but I could see men working with flashlights. So the party had started without me. I hoped Antiay's plan didn't exclude me.

I was thinking about checking out the passageway when I heard a key in the lock. I managed to get behind the door just as it was opening.

I waited until the door closed before I grabbed the shadowy figure, wrapping my arms around her, chest high. I knew before she spoke it was Antiay. I'd have recognized her anywhere. We'd spent many a dark night together.

"Rick! Damn it! You scared the hell out of me. Let go! And get your hands off my breasts!"

"Aw darn, I kind of liked holding you like this."

She turned in my arms, put hers around my neck, kissed me and said, "You're lucky I knew it was you. I might have turned quick and damaged you with my knee."

"Yeah, lucky for both of us."

"You really did startle me. I thought you'd still be sleeping."

"I thought it was you, but I had to make sure. I woke up a couple of minutes ago. I was about to come looking for you."

"I wanted you to sleep as long as possible. They're about to put the drugs from the fishing boat on board. Then they'll transfer the weapons over."

"Good. Can you get your uncle down here now?"

"I think so. He's just sitting there waiting for them to finish. Bobby and the American are taking care of everything."

"Okay. Be careful now—you know what I mean?"

"Yes. I will. Give me a kiss for good luck." I did, and she left.

I checked the action through the porthole and they were still busy out there. Things were going according to plan—their plan that is. It looked like I was down to plan B, which resembled the old Statue of Liberty play in football—the one that almost never worked. Plan C was the old standby—create chaos and run for your lives. Some plan.

I never was much for plans. You could waste a lot of time on them and they hardly ever worked out. In real life you just kept pushing until you found the sore spot and they squealed. But I'd had a plan this time. A damn good one that would maybe have got Antiay and I off this yacht alive. I was gonna be real pissed off—

My train of thought was interrupted by the sound of voices outside the door. I'd have to remember to thank Antiay for the warning. I'd been spacing out and I just had time to duck into the head.

"—had better be important Gretchen. We're right in the middle of—"

"I know, I know Uncle Jurgen." They were in the room now and I heard the door close as she continued. "It's very important—at least to me."

"It had better be because—"

There was a pause, and then the tone of his voice rose almost a full octave. "What is that?"

"It's a gun, dear uncle, as you can see. Now maybe you can tell me why you didn't tell me Victor had been murdered—and who killed him?"

"Gretchen, please, listen, I was going to tell you, but I was waiting for...uh, I was worried about you, so soon after your sister's horrible death. And—"

"And who murdered Victor, Uncle?"

"You can't think I had anything to do with it. I was right here with you. I was happy you were in love. I guess I never told you, but I was planning to help you two get straight—uh, you know, and we'd have a big wedding. I never would have...Gretchen...believe me...you're like a daughter to me. Please put the gun away. It's all that detective's fault— that Sage. If he hadn't been poking around... But how did you know?"

I stepped out of my hiding place. "I told her, pudgy."

A look of shock came over his piggy little doughboy eyes. "You! Sage! What the—" He looked from his niece to me, but it was only an instant before he recovered. "It was his fault, Gretchen." He edged toward her as if it was them against me. "It was him, my dear. Shoot him, quick. I've been investigating. I found out that he saw a photograph of you and Victor together and thought you were her. I think he killed them in a fit of jealousy. He must have argued with Antiay and killed her, and later he shot Victor. The police are about to arrest him. I didn't want to tell you, Gretchen, until it was all over."

He had been edging closer and now he was right in front of her, with the gun barrel right up against his stomach. I didn't move or say anything, and he continued his plea-bargain.

"Gretchen, he's the one you want. Why are you pointing that gun at me? Point it at him." As he said that, he raised his left arm and pointed a stubby white finger at me. It must have distracted her for an instant, and he was very fast for a round guy. He grabbed her gun with his right hand and twisted it out of her grasp. There had been time for her to pull the trigger, but she hesitated, as both her uncle and I had hoped she would. She wasn't a killer after all.

Grossman backed toward the door with the gun trained on me. He motioned for his niece to join me, and she did.

"I don't know how you got on this boat, Sage, but it's evident she is helping you. As for you, Gretchen, my dear, you've created a very difficult—"

"I'm not Gretchen, you bastard, I'm Antiay. You had Gretchen murdered by mistake, and I want to see you die for it."

A shocked expression confused his pudgy features for a moment, then realization clicked in.

"So! I should have known. I knew you were acting strange, but I thought it was the death of your sister. You are Antiay. Of course. You took her place to spy on me. Poor Gretchen. I really am sorry about that. But since she is already dead, my task now becomes simpler. And it really was your fault you know, Mr. Bigtime Detective. Every time you open your mouth, someone dies."

"So you did murder them, Grossman?"

"No, I didn't. Violence is a means of last resort. But I have partners who aren't so particular. You're right about one thing. I know who murdered them. Antiay—Gretchen, what difference? Her death was a stupid mistake. Antiay, did you think I wouldn't have you watched? You threatened me, and you knew too much. I wanted to avoid hurting you, if you minded your own business. Then you took up with this detective. I just wanted to put a scare in you.

"Then the fool botched it. Still, it wouldn't have been necessary if Sage hadn't been snooping around asking all those questions. We didn't know what you might tell him, and I had too much riding on this deal."

"You're the fool, Grossman," I said. "I wasn't investigating anything. Just normal curiosity, and you—"

"No! You! Mr. Detective! It's all your fault. Both of them. You had to keep snooping. You talked to that surfer kid in jail and he told you about Victor. And what does your snooping bring? Another dead body."

"I didn't know anything, you idiot. Like all criminal types, you overreacted."

"Now your snooping around has caused two more deaths. But this time one of the corpses will be yours. You can snoop in hell forever, Sage."

"I wouldn't do that if I were you. We have audio tapes and photographs of you with the head of the DEA. Take a look at these."

I started to reach for my back pocket and he pointed the gun at Antiay.

"Easy, Detective."

I pulled out the packet of photographs Antiay had taken, and tossed them to him. "There is another copy which will be mailed to the cartel if we don't return to La Paz to stop it. All you have to do is tell us who the murderer is—the person working for you who actually pulled the trigger. And let us go. In return, you can go about your business. We want the murderer."

He looked at the photographs, and then he laughed that weird, little, evil doughboy laugh of his.

"You have made a very big mistake, Sage. You see this is my last trip. The weapons business is changing. I already have all the money I need, and soon I'll have a partnership in a new gambling casino. Because of my cooperation against the cartels, your government is helping me with a new identity. Whatever you did cannot hurt me. As for who murdered who, at least you won't have to snoop around to find out who killed you. See what comes from asking too many questions?"

Antiay threw her arms around me as Grossman aimed and squeezed the trigger. I think I even flinched as I heard the click of the firing pin on an empty chamber. It was my turn to laugh as he racked the 9 MM automatic and it clicked again.

"Bang!" I said. "Does that make you feel better?"

"Rick, you beautiful bastard," said Antiay.

But we were rudely interrupted. Powerful searchlights beamed through the portholes and a voice over a loud-hailer blared out heavily accented English, "This is the Navy of Mexico. Stop what you do and drop the weapons!" And then the voice repeated the same sentence in Spanish.

I hugged Antiay, shouting, "At last, our ship has come in!"

My celebration was cut short by the sound of automatic weapons fire, screams, and the clinking of glass as the Mexican Navy spotlights were shot out by someone on the deck of the tuna boat. There was an instant of silence to punctuate Grossman's futile gesture as he threw his hands in the air and screamed, "No, you fools, no, don't shoot."

I still had my hands around Antiay and I dragged her to the deck as the return fire of the Mexican Navy's thirty-caliber machine gun bullets ripped through the fiberglass hull of the *Southern Cross*. Grossman was still standing there with his fat little arms raised in the air, like a caricature of a dead President's victory sign, when the bullet blasted into the whiteness of his gut. His center of gravity was so low that he just stood there for a moment against the door, a look of shock on his face, as the bright red blood oozed onto the front of his all-whiteness, like jelly from a doughnut. Then he fell, and we crawled to his side.

"Sage," he whispered in a familiar death gurgle. "I told you your snooping was going to get somebody killed." He was right, and it shouldn't have happened to a nicer guy.

"Damn, Rick," Antiay said. "Now we'll never know who shot Gretchen."

"There'll be time to worry about that later," I replied. I rolled Grossman's, 'Still Life in an Ever-Growing Pool,' away from the door and reached up and opened it.

We crawled into the passageway just as another exchange of gunfire began. "We've got to get off this boat," I shouted. "If we don't, we'll either be killed or arrested."

"Nice lot of choices you've left us."

"Doing my best, hon. C'mon." I crawled down the passageway toward the stairs to the deck—the same way we'd come, in what seemed like years ago.

At the top of the stairs we waited for a break in the action. "We're going swimming. Follow me—off the side away from the Navy."

"I should hope so. Thanks for warning me this time."

I guessed that meant she was upset with me. But we were still alive. If we stayed that way we'd have time for hurt feelings later.

The gunfire stopped and we crawled into the shelter of the deckhouse. I counted, "one, two and three," and we stood up, climbed to the rail, and executed a beautiful simultaneous dive.

I came up a few feet and a few seconds before Antiay. She was obviously a better swimmer than me underwater, too. I motioned toward the sand spit and the narrow channel dividing *Isla Espíritu Santo* from it's northern mate, *Isla Partida.* She nodded, slipped under the water with hardly a ripple, and I followed.

The next time we surfaced she was even farther ahead of me. I had swum in a half circle, somehow, and when I raised my head out of the water I was facing the *Southern Cross*. There was no moon, but I could make out the Navy ship on the other side of the yacht. The shooting had stopped and the Navy had a hand-held spotlight with which it was searching the decks of the yacht.

I motioned for Antiay to swim on. She waved for me to come, but I waved back violently for her to go ahead. I didn't really want us together in case they sent out a search boat for escapees. If she was ahead of me I could divert them if they saw us.

I motioned again for her to go on, and finally she did. I followed by swimming backward with just my head above the surface. There was no use to my swimming around in circles underwater unless I saw someone in pursuit.

We were at least part of the way to shore before a small launch with a spotlight began to circle the *Southern Cross*. They shined the light half-heartedly in our direction, but I managed to slip under the surface before the beam reached me. I guess Antiay managed to do the same, because the launch continued on around the yacht. I figured they had enough to do that it would be awhile before they made a serious search. I couldn't see Antiay now, but I knew she was safely ahead of me. Something brushed my leg once. Just a fish, I hoped, although paranoia lurked in my mind the rest of the way to shore. I didn't really like swimming at night. I'd seen too many ugly creatures like eels and rays, not to mention sharks, when I'd gone diving in the daylight. At least you could see them then. The more I thought about it, the faster I started to swim and it became difficult not to make noise.

I had just about decided that the danger of the unknown in the deep was almost as bad as the danger from above, when something grabbed me from below and I swear I came out of the water as far as my knees. I started to thrash but then I felt Antiay's body next to mine and she giggled into my ear.

"Jumpy aren't you, Rick?"

"Damn! I could have drowned."

"I doubt it. Put your feet down. It's not much over four feet deep here."

I did. She'd got me.

"I owed you that," she whispered. "It was worth it, too. You nearly jumped all the way out of the water. My big, brave, protector detective."

"Yeah, yeah. Let's get to shore."

"Okay grumpy. Isn't this water great? It's so warm already."

"Yeah, but I don't want to spend the night in it. With this wind blowing the way it is, it's going to be cold when we get out if we can't find shelter. There's an old, abandoned fisherman's *palapa* on shore. Let's head for that."

"Okay."

We floated, with our hands and feet on the sandy bottom in order to keep a low profile. Finally, in barely inches of water, we stopped, laying there for a moment on our bellies, like kids at the beach might on a hot, summer day.

"It's funny, but I feel bad about Uncle Jurgen," said Antiay quietly. "I know he deserved to die, but as far as I know, he was the only relative I had left. I wanted to shoot him back there, but I couldn't pull the trigger."

"I'm glad you didn't, it would have wrecked my plan if he'd found out I'd taken the bullets out of your gun while you were sleeping."

"So you weren't sure I wouldn't shoot him?"

"How could I be? You weren't sure yourself. But I hoped you wouldn't and that he would think you wouldn't. After manipulating you and your sister all of those years, I thought he might feel confident enough to try to get the gun away from you. I just wanted him to feel free to talk. I wouldn't feel sorry for him though. In the end, he intended to shoot both of us."

"You're right of course. I should feel happy he's gone. But it only makes me sad."

"I understand. Let's make a run for the *palapa*. Maybe we can wring out our clothes and get a little dried off. If we get cold, I've got an idea how we can warm up."

"*Mmmmm*. I love those ideas of yours. Let's go."

We stood up and ran. It was a good race but out of the water I was the fastest. Barely.

We reached the *palapa* at a dead run and didn't stop until we were inside. It almost had four walls.

"This is great Antiay. Let me get my lighter out and see what's in here." I was thinking spiders and scorpions, but didn't say it. I always carried a Bic lighter with me, even though I didn't smoke. There'd been a lot of times like this when it had come in handy.

"Thank goodness," a male voice said. I pushed Antiay back through the open door and took a stance.

"Who is it?" I said in my most hostile voice.

"It's me, you idiot. Haven't you had enough fun and games for one night? It's me, and I'm very thankful it's you."

"Hal?" I said as I flicked my Bic. It took three strikes before it lit. The little flame showed Hal huddled in the corner of the *palapa*. "What in the hell are you doing in here?"

Now Antiay was crowding in the doorway behind me. "Rick, you pushed me head over heels." She stared at Hal. "Hal! What are you doing here?"

"I really don't know. I was worried about you guys so I sailed out and anchored on the other side of the sand spit. I felt I had to at least keep an eye on things, in case I could help. I heard all the shooting so I hid in here. I thought you guys were dead for sure. I was about to go back to the boat and sail around to see what I could find out. Then I heard somebody running toward the *palapa* and I thought I was a goner, too. Thank heavens you're both still alive."

Antiay and I just stared at each other open-mouthed. Then, laughing,

I grabbed Hal with my left hand, pulled him to his feet, and we all hugged. Antiay even kissed him a couple of times. "Hal," I said. "You're a work of art. Where's your dinghy?"

Chapter Fifteen

WE FOUND THE dinghy and rowed out to the Harbor Hog. On the way, I told Hal a condensed version of what had happened, and except for a couple of disapproving grunts he rowed in silence. Once we were safely below-deck, he became more talkative.

"Let me get you some dry clothes and a couple of towels," he said. He began to rummage in the forward lockers, and articles of clothing and towels flew at us. "You know you fools are lucky to be alive. Antiay, you shouldn't go around trying to imitate this *macho*. Hey, I understand how you feel—your sister and all, but damn, it'd be a shame to lose both copies of such a beautiful, intelligent womanhood. A damn shame. You better at least let me paint you if you're gonna be—"

"Stop right there, Hal. She's going to be around a long time—I'm making sure of that. So there's no reason for her to sit around naked on this drafty boat for three days catching pneumonia. I appreciate your help and concern, otherwise I'd—"

"Just hold it a minute you two, especially you, Rick. I have something to say about this. I'm flattered you want to paint me Hal. I think it's a great idea—"

"Antiay, damn it—"

"Let me finish, Rick. I said I think it's a great idea and I'd love to have him paint my portrait. That is if you still want to Hal?"

"Of course. Like we talked earlier."

I was beginning to feel like I'd been had again. "You mean you're not talking about a nude painting?"

"Of course not," Hal grinned. "She's a little thin for my style. But she has great cheekbones, and wonderful ears. It's her left ear I really want to capture. Maybe cast among some seashells"

"Oh, Antiay, you're really going to have to pay for this one." I grabbed for her but she ducked behind Hal, who grabbed a paintbrush to hold me off.

"Now Rick, you always said you loved my ears—"

"Yeah, and when I get a hold of you I might just pinch one off."

Hal threw up his hands in mock disgust and said, "Okay, okay, you guys, the deal's off. Now get changed before someone really catches pneumonia. You can have the forward cabin if you promise to behave."

"Yeah well, I'll agree to a truce, but behaving is too much to ask."

"Hey, it was a stupid suggestion. The water tank is full so help yourself to a shower."

We thanked him and made our way forward with the collection of weird clothes he had tossed at us. After our shower, Antiay managed to fit into Hal's paint-speckled jeans okay, and an old sweatshirt. But the best I could do was some kind of Japanese toga thing that made me look like a misfit samurai warrior.

Antiay still hadn't quite forgiven me for the surprises I'd subjected her to back on the *Southern Cross*. So she got in a couple of more jabs. "Rick, with knees like that I'm afraid samurai outfits just aren't going to make a comeback."

"Aw, you always said you liked my legs."

"I used to like your buns, too, but that was before I found out what an asshole you are."

"Hon, look, I'm sorry I had to keep you in the dark back there." I pulled her into my arms. "I'll try to make it up to you. It's just that I'm used to working on my own. And the governor wasn't even sure he could get the Navy here at all."

She pulled away and went back to combing her hair. "That's not much of an excuse. I don't think you trusted me. What about taking the bullets out of my gun without telling me?"

"Yeah, well, you didn't tell me about the gun. I didn't want you to kill him, so I unloaded it while you were sleeping. I wanted to find out who was working for him, and to do that I needed our little scene to be believable. It's not that I didn't trust you. I knew how you felt because two days ago I felt the same way. Anyway, it worked."

"How can you say that? We still don't know who the killer was."

"I'm not so sure. Your uncle told us how and why it happened."

"We'd guessed that."

"Yeah, but he said something that almost lit a light in some dusty corner of my tiny little brain. Except that with all the excitement I can't quite remember what it was. And if you're going to stay mad at me I'll never be able to concentrate on remembering it."

"That sounds like a dirty trick. I'm not really mad at you. Maybe just a little peeved that you pulled it off all by yourself. You didn't even need me."

I pulled her to me once again. "You're wrong about that. Until we teamed up, I was only managing to get my head kicked around, like a punted football in a low-scoring game. I was behind at least six to nothing until you signed with my team. Just not having you smack me in the head with a rum bottle is a lot."

"Yeah, I forgot about that. I guess maybe we're even after all."

"Great. Now let's go see if Hal has any food aboard. I'm kind of hungry."

HAL WAS ONE step ahead of us. "I thought you guys might be hungry after all the excitement. It's just bachelor sailor food—a Cup-O-Noodles and Irish coffee, but at least it's hot."

I was hungry enough I could have eaten a Cup-O-Mud. "Well, at three-twenty a.m., after a full night of death and destruction, I always like a good hot Cup-O-Noodles, but it's the Irish whiskey that's really going to hit the spot. Maybe I could have a Cup-O-Whiskey and some noodles-coffee?"

"I don't know about the noodles in your coffee, Rick. How about a Cup-O-Noodles and you mix your own Irish coffee?"

"Sounds like a deal."

"How about you Antiay?"

"I'm not so fussy as Rick. Whatever you've got sounds great. I'm fading fast so I hope you'll excuse me if I nod off before my noodles cool."

"We don't stand on ceremony on the Harbor Hog, Antiay. Just make yourself at home. If you want, you can take your noodles and coffee forward and eat in your bunk."

"Gee, that sounds great. You sure you guys wouldn't mind? I think I must have used up a year's worth of adrenaline tonight, and I didn't get a lot of sleep last night either." She gave me a wink and a smile.

"Go on, Antiay. I think I'll drink some whiskey with Hal before I come to bed. That way maybe you can finally get some sleep."

"Okay. Goodnight you two heroes of mine."

I was still feeling wired after the action on the *Southern Cross*. I was used to not getting much sleep in the middle of a case. There were a lot of times I'd only had three or four hours a night for weeks on end. And losing a little beauty rest wasn't going to do me too much damage anyway. Antiay was quite a different matter.

Hal and I were well into our third Irish coffee when the sun came up and reminded me about the five W's—who, what, why, where and when. I told him about it, and he said, "Don't forget 'whew!'"

"Or wow and whoopie."

"Hey, we better stop there Rick. Speaking of what, though, I know where there's a great lobster hole just around the point. What do you say we dinghy over there and check it out. It'd make for a great lunch when we wake up. Or are you in a hurry to get back to La Paz?"

"Sounds fine. We're not in any hurry. We have some unfinished business back there but it can wait. In fact I need a little time to contemplate the situation."

"If I were you, I'd take a lot of time to contemplate. In fact the world would be a much better place if everyone did it."

"Yeah well, it's kind of like those lobsters. If we just sit around here contemplating them, we'd soon run out of beer to wash them down with."

"You've got a point there, somewhere, Rick. Let's go."

He got out the spotlights, snorkels, masks and fins, and we loaded them in his high-speed Avon dinghy.

On the way over, he told me about his special spot. "Hey, wait 'till you see this place Rick. It's a huge underwater cave. The entrance is about sixteen feet down at high tide, so it'll be a little less now. It's weird because the cave actually gets about five feet deeper at the back. You can surface inside even at high tide. The first time I found it, I was scuba diving, but I've gone in there several times since, free-diving. It's a little scary at first, but now I know it as well as I know my boat. You can wait for me outside if you want to."

"No, I have to see it. It can't be any worse than the day we went diving at the sea lion rookery."

"You mean when that bull charged you in the arch?" He started to laugh.

"Yeah that. He thought I was after his woman, but she really wasn't my type. That fish-breath—ugh!"

I hoped today would be different. I was brave enough in most situations, I thought. But I was no superhero in the water. I hoped I could avoid any situation that might make me the star performer in another of Hal's cartoon fantasies. It was going to be bad enough when Antiay got around to telling how I'd nearly walked on water last night.

The dive was uneventful. The cave was every bit as beautiful and scary as Hal had said it was. There were lobsters everywhere and at least one large eel grinning at us. We hooked three large lobsters out of around twenty we saw, and each of them weighed over three pounds. I was already drooling as we exited the cave. We swam around awhile outside and saw two more lobsters making their way back to holes after a night of foraging. Finally we swam back to the dinghy and headed for the Harbor Hog. By seven o'clock I was climbing into the bunk next to Antiay, and by seven-o-three I was asleep.

I WOKE UP a few minutes after Noon, to the smell of freshly brewed coffee and the sound of the anchor chain flaking itself into the locker. Hal evidently had us underway.

Antiay was curled up spoon-wise around my back, and either she had awakened, too, or her fingers were sleepwalking around turtle cove. "Be careful that turtle doesn't bite you," I warned.

"Yes, he's a big one isn't he? But I'm not afraid of turtles, and he seems quite friendly. See, I can feel him coming out of his shell already."

She was right of course, so I rolled over and we played ocean for a while. Then we showered and joined Hal in the cockpit.

"Ah, the happy campers have arisen. Rick, you know where the cups are. Grab some coffee, and I'll have a little more, too, if you don't mind."

I got us all coffee and handed it around. "You should have woke me to give you a hand, Hal."

"Nah, it's all routine for me. I was afraid the anchor chain might wake you up, but I thought it was time we got underway."

"It was simply a wonderful way to wake up, wasn't it Rick?"

"You can say that again. Hal and I have a surprise for you Antiay." I told her about the lobster cave.

"Darn, I wish I had been able to see it. But I really was tired. I can't believe you two actually went swimming after last night. And in a cave—especially you Rick." She gave me a mischievous grin that threatened for a moment to spill out the story of my panic in the deep, but she held back after she knew I knew I owed her one.

Hal noted the exchange and smiled, but let it pass. Sort of. "It seems there's more than just a lot of bull in your sea stories, Rick," he said.

"Yeah well, maybe I should get those lobster cooking, what do you think Hal?"

"Why don't you take the wheel instead? I know where everything is. Besides, I'm sort of enjoying being in charge of a honeymoon cruise."

I took the wheel, happily, and Antiay leaned against me inside my free arm. It was a beautiful day with a nice steady breeze, and the tri-maran sailed like a flying carpet. There wasn't a cloud in the sky, but in my mind, thunderheads kept crowding the horizon.

After a while, Hal signaled we were ready to eat and we put the Harbor Hog on automatic pilot, clinked glasses in a toast to creatures of the oceans, and ate a lobster lunch so perfect even the most jaded billionaire would have envied us.

As perfect as it was, none of us could shake the contrast of violent death behind us and its huge shadow lurking ahead. We were three friends seated at a dinner table floating in the eye of a storm—the clear blue of sub-tropical sky overhead, the deeper blue of the sea below, and the encircling darkness of uncontrollable forces. We smiled and offered toasts to peaceful times and to each other, but it was more to strengthen resolve than for quiet satisfaction, and the clinks our glasses made were swept away by the wind.

When we had finished, Hal insisted on cleaning up by himself. So Antiay took the wheel, and I wandered forward to be alone and try to make some sense of it all.

I leaned back against a full sailbag and thought about the senseless murder of Antiay's sister. Grossman had said it was my fault. They intended to have Antiay falsely arrested because I had been asking questions, and they were afraid she would tell me about Grossman's business. They knew I had connections to the governor and maybe they were even afraid I was working for him. They had counted on Antiay's loyalty to her sister to keep her from identifying the real person in the picture. And of course the other individual in the photographs was the governor's son, Victor. A double-barreled attack.

On the other hand, if we all played ball the charges would be dropped and files would disappear. A good plan except someone botched the job.

Was it my fault? No. Murderers always tried to rationalize their crimes. They'd say, "If she'd only done what I told her," or "all I wanted was the money" or a thousand other such excuses, including blaming their mothers. Funny thing, no jury had ever convicted a mother for the murder her son had committed.

No, it wasn't my fault I had stumbled into the midst of crimes about to be committed. But how did they know me well enough to be afraid of my questions? White? Possibly. I'd got in the way of one of his operations before, when he'd tried to cover up murder to save a drug bust. But that time he was covering for an informer in order to use him. I didn't think White would actually stoop to murder. Still, Grossman said they hadn't intended to murder Antiay/Gretchen. And there was no one else who knew me, except maybe someone around the governor. Maybe they'd bribed Rafael Flores, the governor's assistant. Another possibility.

I smacked myself in the head. Damn. I wasn't much closer than I had been before we came out here. If only Grossman had told me who. At least he was out of the way now. With the driving force gone, the rest was mop-up. Trouble was, from experience I knew that could be the most dangerous part of a case. People became even more desperate.

Damn it, there was something I couldn't remember. I smacked myself in the head again. Something Grossman said that made me feel I knew who the killer was. I had been trying to remember since last night, but it must have been something I hadn't paid attention to at the time. My subconscious mind registered it though, and now it felt like a dream I was trying to remember.

I guess I started to smack myself again, because a hand caught my wrist in motion. "Rick," Antiay said, "Stop beating up on yourself. Don't you think your poor head has taken enough abuse? I don't want to be stuck loving some punch-drunk guy who can't even remember my name."

I pulled her down so she was laying with her head across my chest. "Don't worry. I could never forget a beautiful name like...uh...um...don't tell me...oh...it's right on the tip of my—"

"Here, put this on the tip of your stupid nose." She doubled up her fist as if to hit me.

"Antiay! It's Antiay. A truly beautiful name to go with a truly beautiful person."

"That's more like it, Rick. Now quit teasing and give me a kiss."

I did, and we lay there together trying to pretend we hadn't a care in the world. Finally though, she admitted her true feelings. "I have a really bad feeling and I'm not sure why."

"What do you mean?"

"I don't know...it's like a foreboding or something. Like intuition, or fear of the dark when you're alone in the woods. Or maybe...I don't know...like a premonition."

"You've been through some bad times in the last week. It's bound to take a toll on your outlook."

"I suppose...probably that's it. I hope so. But promise me you'll be really careful, will you? I couldn't stand to lose you, too. Please?"

"Sure. Don't worry, hon. I'll be careful. I read somewhere that ninety percent of the people who get bit by rattlesnakes are people who are trying to kill the snake. But they're also people who forget how dangerous a cornered rattlesnake can be. I haven't forgotten that. Still, when you've got a rattler under your bed you've got to get him out and I'm very well trained to do it. Don't forget, it's my job. I'm a professional. It's the amateurs who get bit, unfortunately."

"I know, but I can't seem to shake this bad feeling I've got. I'm scared, Rick."

"Okay, I understand. I promise you, I'll try to let the authorities handle it if I can—once I know for sure who did it. All right?"

"Yes. I love you."

"I love you, too."

We sailed most of the rest of the way in silence. I wished I had been able to make her feel better. I kicked myself a couple of times for the stupid rattlesnake analogy. She wanted to be reassured and I bring up death from poisonous snakes. *Great Rick, some comfort you are.*

But the truth was, I had the same ominous feeling she did, and I couldn't shake it either. On top of that, the weather started to turn nasty just as we entered the La Paz channel. We watched as a towering thunderhead circled the mountains to the south and converged on La Paz. The first major storm of the year, it carried no rain. Instead it sucked up dust and hurled it toward us. A *chubasco,* they call it. I hoped it wasn't an omen. I usually didn't believe in that kind of thing, but today I wasn't so sure. In a *chubasco* the wind swirls and comes at you violently from every direction. Before the first of the dust storm reached us, Hal called out to drop the sails. We managed to get everything tied down before the fifty-knot winds struck us, and we huddled in the cockpit as the dirt and sand pelted us like dry rain.

It didn't take long for the *chubasco* to blow itself out, and twenty minutes later all that was left of its violence was a thin layer of dust everywhere on the boat, and heat lightning flashing in the remaining thunderheads to the south.

"Hey," Hal said, "this trail driving gives you a powerful thirst don't it pardners? How about you pop us open three cold ones, Rick, and we'll wash down the dust of the herd while we mosey on down to the ranch?"

We all laughed and I got the beers. "Here's to moseying home," I said, and we clunked our bottles in a toast.

"How about a campfire song?" Antiay said, and we began singing "Bumba deeda, bumba deeda, bumba deeda...Happy trails...to you...until... we meet...again..."

It was a rousing rendition that continued right on in to the dock at the *Marina de La Paz*. We even heard a couple of answering yee-ha's as we tied up.

Antiay and I both felt a little better as we thanked Hal for his wonderful hospitality and for rescuing us from the beach. "Aw shucks, it was nothing," he said as we started up the dock. "But guys, be careful, okay?"

He gave us both a hug before he turned around and climbed back on the boat. We waved goodbye and continued up the dock.

"He sure is a nice guy," Antiay said when we were out of earshot.

"Yeah, he's a work of art all right. That's for sure."

At the gate of the Marina, we hailed the cab parked in front of *Molinos* bar and restaurant. Steve was at his place by the gate and as we passed him I asked, "Going to rain tonight Steve?"

"Nah," he answered as I dropped some pesos into his can. "But watch out for lightning."

"Thanks for the info," I said as we got into the taxi.

At my house we showered, drank coffee, and watched the deep red sunset. "Must be the dust from the storm making that color," I said.

"Yes, probably. You know, I really hadn't thought about it much until now, but all of my things are on the *Southern Cross*. Gretchen's and mine. I'll have to go shopping. I can't go around in your oversized bowling shirts forever."

"Hey, I think you look great. Especially with nothing else on."

"Oh-oh, that does it. Didn't I have a pair of jeans around here somewhere?"

"Yeah, they're on the hook in the far closet. But—"

She wasn't listening to me, and came back with the jeans on. "Rick, you did say you had to go and see the governor, didn't you?"

"Yeah, I guess so, but—"

"We'll have time for that later, when you're not in such a hurry."

"Yeah, well, the governor could wait, too, but I guess you're right. I better give him a call."

I dialed the number, and when Flores answered, I said, "Mogote."

"Oh, it's you, *Señor Sage*. The governor is anxious to speak to you."

"Yeah, me, too. But not over the telephone. I can be there in half an hour if that's agreeable."

"Just a minute, I'll check with him."

There was a click as it went on hold, and a couple of minutes later it clicked again. "That's fine. The governor will see you in thirty minutes."

"*Hasta luego*," I said and hung up the phone wondering why I hadn't given myself at least an hour. The lovely influence of Antiay, no doubt.

"He's going to see me in a half-hour," I told her. "Maybe I can get him to let you get your things off the yacht."

"That would be great, although I really don't want to go back there again."

"Maybe I can get them to box the stuff up and deliver it."

"That would be nice. I'm afraid I've lost the terrible anger I felt after Gretchen's death. Seeing Uncle Jurgen die didn't make me feel any better. It didn't bring her back. I just want to bury the dead now, including all of the memories—at least for a while."

"I don't blame you. You could take a nap until I get back."

"Maybe I'll do just that."

"Oh, before you do though, would you call Freddy for me? Give him a condensed version of what has happened and tell him I need to see him. Tell him I'll stop by after I see the governor."

"All right, Rick. I wish this could all wait for tomorrow though. You haven't forgotten your promise have you?"

"No, of course not. But the person responsible for your sister's and Victor's deaths, is probably a little jumpy right now. We might be able to flush him out. I have a vague feeling I should already know who it is—it could come to me at any moment. Anyway, I have to report in to the governor and explain what happened out there. With the DEA being involved, he needs all the info he can get."

"I understand. Just please be careful. I'm still scared something terrible is going to happen."

"Don't worry. As long as I know you're safe here, I'm not going to take any risks. I'm looking forward to coming home tonight."

I kissed her and grabbed a shirt from the closet—the midnight-blue one. The name over the pocket says, Bob. On the back it reads, 'Santa Monica Bowl – Have a ball with the stars,' and there are ten stars in a triangle. What can I say? It was a gift from a friend named Bob who lives in Santa Monica. And it was a nice color.

I said goodbye to Antiay, and fired up the Hog. It always made me feel good to hear the rumble of all those horses between my legs. If that's macho, then here's to it.

I rode slowly toward the governor's mansion, which was on the beach at the opposite end of town—on the way to Pichilingue. Couples were already strolling beneath the palm trees along the *Malecón*. The bay was dead calm, but there was still lightning flashing on the other side near *San Juan de la Costa*, the big phosphate mine. La Paz was trying hard to live up to her reputation as Baja Sur's City of Peace. She was putting up a brave front. It was hard to believe that somewhere behind this facade lurked a multiple murderer. Hard to believe even for me, partly because I didn't want to. If the day ever came when I didn't feel a little shocked that a human being could willfully commit a violent crime against another human being—well, I just hoped there would never be such a time.

The ride took me past Freddy's office and I regretted again that I hadn't given myself time to talk to him before I saw the governor. It wasn't critical. Now that Grossman's operation was destroyed, the governor could probably tell me what I wanted to know about his assistant, Flores.

On the outskirts of town I opened the throttle a bit and the Hog snorted like a huge sow contentedly feeding her piglets. I knew that another twist of that throttle could turn her into a mad mamma, but I resisted the urge, reminding myself that this wasn't a pleasure trip.

A couple of minutes later I pulled up to the guard shack at the entrance to the governor's palace. A guard stepped out to greet me.

"*Buenos noches Señor,*" he said.

"*Buenos noches,*" I replied. "*Soy Rick Sage. Tengo una cita con El Gorernador.*"

"*Sí, Señor* Sage. *El Gorernador te está esperando. Pasa con mi amigo.*"

He pointed to another guard who pointed to a parking space. I parked the bike in the place he had pointed out, and followed him inside to a small office that was evidently used for such clandestine encounters. The guard left me sitting in one of the leather chairs and then exited back out through the same door we had used to enter. No doubt he would be standing guard there.

I barely had time to gaze around the room when another door opened and the governor entered, alone. That was good.

I stood up, reaching out to shake his hand, but he pulled me to him, embracing me warmly—like a long lost brother. "*Buenos noches, Rick,*" he said. "*Cómo esta?*"

"*Bien,*" I replied, "and you?" It was time to switch to English before my Spanish ran out. He obliged me.

"I am fine, Rick. Very, very fine. My friend, you didn't tell me there would be shooting at the island. One of our sailors was wounded, though not seriously, *Gracias a Dios.* Please have a seat."

We sat down as I replied, "Who would have thought they'd be so stupid?"

"Yes, who indeed. This time it seems to have worked to our advantage however. A routine patrol encounters smugglers and is fired upon. Piracy in these times—it is outrageous. Our national honor has been violated. And to find out your Government was secretly involved in an operation on our territory. It was all we could do to cover up such an arrogant act. If our press got word of that, why the relations between our two great nations might have been irreparably damaged. And so on."

"I see, Governor. Then everything has gone well?"

"Oh, very well indeed. It couldn't have been better. Now please, tell me what you know."

I told him everything that had happened since I'd last seen him, and he listened intently without interrupting. When I finished he leaned back in his chair and thought about what I'd said for a couple of minutes before he spoke. "It was lucky that you and your friend managed to get off the yacht undetected. And a lucky shot from our Navy to rid us of *Señor* Grossman. It seems we have been very lucky indeed. I can assure you that this *Señor* White, the head of the DEA, is about to retire. And the person most responsible for the deaths of the lady and my son—this *Señor* Grossman—he is now dead himself. Tomorrow I am going to announce that we are issuing a trial license for a gambling casino to a *grupo* from Cabo San Lucas. We have decided that La Paz is not an appropriate place for such an operation. So you see my friend, everything has worked out. Perhaps we should not press our luck, if you know what I mean?"

"I think I do sir, but I'm afraid I can't agree. There is still a murderer loose and I intend to find out who he is and bring him to justice. If he thinks he has gotten away with murder, I assure you he will kill again, sooner or later. After all, for all his trouble, he has achieved nothing."

"Perhaps you are right. In any event, I owe you a great deal and I'll do anything in my power to help you."

"Thanks."

"No. Thank you. Now...You do not yet know who the killer is?"

"Well no, not exactly. I have all of the pieces to the puzzle. I'm sure of that. Now I just have to make them fit. It's a process of elimination. One possibility is someone high up in your office who may have been bribed. What about *Señor* Flores, your assistant?"

"I can see why you might suspect him. There is a lot of money to be made from this casino, it is true. But there is even more money to be made from investments in real estate in the area it is to be located in. That is why I can assure you that you can cross Flores off your list of suspects. His family has a major interest in the *grupo* to which the license is now going. And they also control considerable real estate in the Cabo area. He has always lobbied strongly against the Grossman interests."

"Yeah well, like I said, it's a process of elimination. Tell me, has anyone else contacted you about any of this in the past few days?"

"You mean about the casino license specifically?"

"That, or anything to do with this case—the murders, me, anything?"

"Someone out of the usual you mean...*hmmm*...no. I don't think so. There was a call, but that was a condolence call—for Victor. Other than—"

"Who called about Victor?"

"That detective friend of yours. I forget his name...Alfredo something."

"Freddy? Fast Freddy?"

"Yes, that's how he is called by some people. He was a friend of Victor's. Remember, you had him pick up Victor at the airport when you sent him back from Los Angeles after that trouble he was in. You said you wanted to make sure he got all the way home. They became friends after that. Alfredo called to say he was sorry about Victor's death. He wanted to know if he could help in any way."

"When was that? When did he call?"

"I think it was the day after I talked to you at the dam."

A light was starting to dawn inside my head. A very bright, burning light. My voice actually quavered a bit. "What else did he say...as exactly as you can remember?"

"Let's see...he asked if I had any idea who might have killed Victor. I told him an investigation was under way. He said again that he'd like to help, for Victor's sake. I told him that you were investigating it for me and if he wanted to help he should contact you. Then he offered his condolences again, and that was all. Other than that I can't think of anyone else who called."

The dawning light in my head had turned to fireworks with sirens and bells. Freddy and Victor—friends! I hadn't known that and Freddy hadn't told me. Stop-action frames began to flip through my mind. Grossman saying, *You talked to that kid in the jail and he told you about Victor.*

Flip. Another frame. No one knew the surfer kid had told me about Victor except Freddy. I saw myself telling him that I was flying to Mazatlán to see Victor. He must have left right away—to beat me to him.

Flip. Victor's friend Freddy secretly taking pictures at a cocaine party. Or maybe he just arranged to have them taken.

Flip. Freddy planting evidence at Antiay's apartment, being surprised by Gretchen and murdering her—thinking it was Antiay.

Flip. Me talking to Freddy before Antiay's death—about the hotel on the Mogote and the *Southern Cross.* That's what Grossman meant when he said it was my fault. Too many questions, he'd said. Damn. I'd accidentally spooked Freddy. Just innocent curiosity.

Flip. Me telling Antiay to call Freddy. Damn again.

I jumped to my feet—maybe only seconds had passed but it seemed like years were wasting.

"What is it, Rick?" the governor said, and I saw my shock reflected in his face.

"It's Freddy! Alfredo! He's the killer. I've got to stop him."

"Alfredo? Are you sure?"

"I don't have time to explain," I said. "Can you get the police to his office and his condo?"

"Yes, of course, but—"

"Don't use the *federales.* He's got connections with them. Here—" I wrote down Freddy's addresses and the number of Pepe's friend, the chief prosecutor. "Let him know please. He's a good man."

He picked up the paper and looked at it. "Yes, of course. I know him. He is a very good man. He knows about this matter?"

"Yes. He said he'd help."

"Good. Then we can search the areas."

"Thanks. And warn your men—he's armed and dangerous. Can you send someone to the airport in case he tries to fly out?"

"Of course."

"I have to use your telephone."

"Yes, go ahead."

I dialed the number and waited while it rang at least ten times. I set the handset back down slowly as my mind whirled. Something was wrong. I had to get there fast—alone.

"I've got to go," I said as I ran out the door. I jumped on the Hog and peeled out past the guard who tried to stop me.

I FELT LIKE a cartoon version of reality, riding a slow-motion rocket along the *Malecón* trying desperately to get somewhere I couldn't possibly get to fast enough.

The traffic got heavy with cruisers near the downtown, and finally stopped altogether. I searched for a ramp, found one, swerved onto the sidewalk and raced along, ducking palm fronds and honking at strolling lovers who scrambled out of my way, shocked once again at the behavior of crazy *gringos.*

I didn't care. I didn't care about anything except that Antiay should be alive and safe. The traffic thinned and I jumped the bike back to the street and sped along, passing cars on both sides and straining my eyes to see ahead into the dark shadows for dogs or small boys who might race across my path unexpectedly.

I ran red lights and I was lucky. I had to brake only once—for a wide-turning semi I swerved around. I wasn't afraid of collision because I was heading for one. Freddy was an intelligent guy and he'd know I'd guess his secret sooner or later. Everything fit now. He tried to kill me twice already; probably hired someone to do the drive-by shooting, but Freddy had to have been the guy in the baseball cap, driving the pick-up that tried to run me off the road on the way to Cabo San Lucas.

Two more botched murder attempts. I wasn't so easy to kill, but he was determined to cover his tracks. What a mess, Freddy. Greed will get you every time. I wished it hadn't been him, but there was no doubt.

My mind was whirling so I made myself concentrate as I pulled off the main road onto my dirt street. I got up some speed and coasted to within half a block. There was some unfinished construction on the corner and I pushed the Hog in behind the wall.

My heart raced as I saw Freddy's car parked in front of my place. Damn, my worst fears. But he didn't know I knew, because he hadn't hidden his car. Maybe I could carry on a bluff—let him think I suspected Flores or someone. Let him think he had a chance to get out of town.

Yeah well, I could stand out here and make plans all night, but nothing was going to happen until I walked through that door. So I did.

"Welcome to the party, my friend," he said as I entered. I had been wrong. Freddy was ready this time. He held a gun on Antiay, who had been crying.

"Freddy, if you've hurt her—"

"Don't worry, she's just a little sad. She'll be okay as long as you do what I say. Now lift your shirt so I can be sure you don't have the big gun on you."

I did as he said, turning all the way around. "Are you all right Antiay?" She nodded yes. "Why'd you do it Freddy?"

"For the big dollars, why else? They promised me to share in the casino. I did some work for the *cabrónes* from Las Vegas once and they liked the results."

"They're not gonna like the results this time."

"I'm afraid you are right. It is as the T-shirt says, 'Shit Happens.' You have caused me much problems, Rick."

"It's all your own fault. Now you're only making it worse. The governor knows about it. The police are searching your place right now. Let Antiay go and I promise I'll help you get out of town."

"I'm afraid not my friend. Since you've opened your big mouth again, I'll have to take her along to guarantee my safety. But look at it this way—I was going to kill you both. Now, if you cooperate, perhaps that won't be necessary."

"I won't help you unless you let Antiay go."

"That is okay, I don't really need you. I know you, Rick. You didn't tell anyone you were coming here. No, I am sure of that. So understand me well, my friend. I didn't intend to kill Antiay, only to cause her some problems, and some for the governor to make him cooperative. You see, *mi amigo*, the joke is on you. It was all a big mistake, a coincidence, as you like to say. She recognized me and I had no choice but to get rid of her. You should be happy it turned out to be her sister. For me, however, killing is killing. Victor was easier. One or two more is no difference."

Antiay kicked at him, but he evaded her as she sobbed, "You evil bastard. We were your friends."

"Antiay! Don't!" I shouted. "Just do what he tells you."

"That is good advice, Rick. A millionaire has many friends. Now sit down in that chair."

I did as he said, and he ordered Antiay to cut the cord from the drapes. Afterwards he had her tie my ankles to the chair, while he tied my hands behind me and gagged me.

"Antiay is coming with me. If I get out of La Paz, I promise you she will live. *Adios*, my friend."

He pushed Antiay out the door and I started to work on my bindings. I was a regular Houdini at escapes. I'd practiced that kind of thing, as a hobby I thought went well with detective work. I'd spent long hours on stakeout escaping from my own handcuffs, until it was as easy as taking off a pair of gloves. Rope was even easier. I even did escapes to entertain friends sometimes. Luckily, I'd never done them for Freddy.

They probably weren't even in the car before I was loose. I dove for the cannon hidden in the hole, checked to make sure it was loaded, racked a round into the chamber, and ran out the door. They were just pulling away. I ran to the gate, crept out into the poorly lit street, and made for the bike. I had her roaring down the street after them before their taillights were out of sight.

I left my lights off and hung back. They were driving at a reasonable speed so as not to attract attention. I was sure Antiay was driving and I just hoped she wouldn't try anything reckless. Freddy didn't really have a plan, I was sure. He was making it up as he went along, and there was no telling at what point he might decide to shoot her and go it alone.

They drove northward on the highway, passing the white statue marking the entrance to La Paz. It's a forty-foot high sculpture of a whale's tail that, viewed from another perspective, becomes a white dove. A symbol of peace Freddy had tarnished. I was surprised it didn't fall down when he drove past.

If he was going to make a try for the airport, hoping they hadn't been notified, maybe I'd be able to sneak up on him while he was distracted by the police I knew were waiting there. It was my best chance, and sure enough they took the turnoff to the airport.

Half-way there his brake lights flashed, and in a moment I saw the reason. Police lights were flashing all over the airport parking lot. I couldn't blame them, even as I cursed them. They didn't want to sneak up on an armed and dangerous killer. The pay was way too low.

Then there were more flashing lights coming from way behind us, and Freddy's car suddenly turned off, racing down a dirt road away from the airport.

Damn! Freddy's plans had changed again. The only option left to him was to try to get as far as he could across-country. Then he could get rid of Antiay, ditch the car and try to melt into the countryside. That's what he should have done in the first place, but he'd panicked. La Paz was surrounded by a wilderness of cactus and mesquite. It wouldn't be that hard for a Mexican to disappear.

Trouble was, I knew the road he'd turned onto. It ended in huge fields of marigolds, grown commercially for dye. The fields were managed by a friend of mine named Pedro. He'd taken me there once when they were in blossom. Freddy wasn't going to get far down that road, and I was afraid of what he'd do when he got to the end.

I turned down the road, following. It was all I could do. They speeded up and I tried to respond, but the dirt road was rough, and my Hog was no dirt bike.

They pulled away from me, disappearing for a moment around a bend in the road. Now it was no more than a quarter of a mile to the fields so I maintained my speed. Sure enough, once around the bend I could see them entering the field at about fifty miles an hour.

Suddenly they stopped, hitting the soft earth with the engine screaming and the wheels spinning as a cloud of dust filled the bright beams of his headlights.

Antiay got out of the car and ran farther into the marigolds, but Freddy was right behind her. She fell and he stood aiming the gun at her as she started to get up. Afraid he might kill her, I decided to give him no choice but to deal with me first. I gunned the Hog straight at him.

He heard me and turned, looking a bit surprised his hostage gambit hadn't worked. He brought the gun up, and I watched him aiming all in slow motion as I rode full-throttle straight at him. In fast-frame succession I saw the flame in the muzzle, felt the windshield shatter, and heard his curse as I rode him down, feeling the thud and the motorcycle cartwheeling in a shower of dirt and marigolds and wetness.

I don't know how long I was out. Not long, because I woke covered in dirt and marigolds, with the feel of raindrops splashing onto my face. Then I realized my head was cradled in Antiay's lap and the raindrops were her tears.

"Oh baby, baby, you're alive," she said.

"Am I?" I asked. "That's good."

"Yes, that's very good," she said as she kissed me.

I lay there a few seconds as things started to come back. "Freddy?" I asked.

"Dead," she said. "Crushed by the Hog."

"The bike!" I said, trying to get up. Somehow the marigolds seemed to prevent it, the scent growing heavy as waves of pain ran up my leg.

"Your leg is under the motorcycle," I heard her say through a thickening fog, "and you've been shot through the shoulder. I've slowed down the bleeding but you must be quiet. They're coming now."

Then there were flashing lights, and people speaking words I couldn't understand, so I closed my eyes, slipping off into the marigold mist, mumbling, "La Paz—such a quiet little place."

Epilogue

"FIFTY-ONE," SHE called out as I finished another lap in my pool.

Antiay had trained me nearly back to normal. It had been six weeks since I'd ridden Freddy down in that Marigold field, and the broken leg was almost normal. The broken ribs still gave me a bit of trouble occasionally, if I turned wrong, but I had most of my wind back from the punctured lung. My swimming had never been pretty anyway. And luckily the bullet had missed most of the crucial stuff in my shoulder so it, too, was doing well.

"Fifty-two." This time with more than a hint of the taskmaster in her voice. "You're slowing down, Rick. You'll never get there if you don't pick it up a bit. This is your last chance to show me how tough you are."

I picked it up, at least producing more splash. I was having trouble concentrating, but it hadn't much to do with my swimming technique. This was our last day together in La Paz. It hadn't been the same for either of us since finding out Freddy had murdered Antiay's sister, by mistake. She felt guilty. It should have been her, but her sister had died instead. She would never get over it, I knew. For the rest of her life she would replay the events in her head, at every turning point thinking how she might have done something differently that would have changed the outcome. But she couldn't change it, of course, and the tape would always end in the same gruesome way; finding her sister's body laying there without a—

"Fifty-three. That was a bit better Rick, and your buns are wonderful, but a little more technique and a little less splash would be good."

As if there were any chance of that. I would keep splashing up and down the pool, just like we would both never quite get over Freddy's betrayal and her sister's death. That was the horrible thing about murder. It left a memory without an ending, like an infinity-symbol tattooed on your brain. For a long while Antiay would try to go backwards to a time before Gretchen's death, but everything would eventually bring her once again to that horrible night in La Paz. It was ironic that La Paz, the city whose name in Spanish meant peace, would never give her any. Neither would she find peace with me, at least for awhile. Our love had been sidetracked in the culmination of her nightmare. Once her sister had been avenged, all of her hatred evaporated, like the last of drops of water spilled in hot sand. But she could not rid herself of the sadness.

"Fifty-four."

I heard it in her voice that time, and I snuck a peek at her during my breath stroke. Even with that sad smile she was beautiful. She had tried to get her old self back, and for short periods she could almost do it. But it took way too much effort. I had tried everything I could think of to take her mind off it, but I was too much a part of what happened. For awhile, we had talked about her going back to Los Angeles with me, but every day it became clearer that wouldn't work, either. It was me who finally said it. That she probably needed some time alone.

Reluctantly, she agreed. Being Jurgen Grossman's only living relative, she needed to sort out his finances, which meant traveling to various countries where he'd hidden his wealth. She wanted to recover what she could and set up a trust in Gretchen's name, for some worthy cause she hadn't quite decided upon yet. I told her that was a wonderful idea, and she could join me in Los Angeles later.

"Fifty-five. Looking good Rick."

Yeah well. Out of this entire mess, one good thing had happened. Because of all the bad publicity about the big shoot-up with Grossman's boat out at the island, the Baja casino deal had been canceled, at least for awhile. Gunrunning and drug-smuggling, and shooting at the Mexican Navy, all with a U.S. Government Agent on board the pirate vessel, had sunk even an all-Mexican casino deal. Bill White, the DEA guy, had been recalled to Washington, and it looked like his career was over. That was some satisfaction at least.

"Sixty-nine," Antiay said, totally blowing my rhythm. I swallowed some water trying to breathe in the wrong place, and pulled up in the middle of the pool, spluttering.

She came over and sat on the edge of the pool, her legs dangling in the water. I looked in her shimmering blue eyes and I could see we were both thinking along the same lines. Passion could still distract us from the bad memories. Was it wrong we had started using it in order to forget everything else?

Nah.

I did a froggy kick, drifting over to rest between her legs. I looked up and she ran her hands through my hair, and kissed me. I kissed her back, sliding down around her curves at the breathtakingly slow pace of a hot Baja afternoon, pulling her to me as I hummed a juicy mango tune....

~ * ~

Murdoch Hughes

Murdoch Hughes and his wife Jan lived for over six years in La Paz, Mexico, writing and cruising their sailboat, Hunter Star, throughout the many uninhabited islands in the Sea of Cortez.

Printed in the United States
18910LVS00001BA/76-165